# SWIMMING IN THE MONSOON SEA

# SHYAM SELVADURAI

≋ ≋ ≋

# SWIMMING IN THE MONSOON SEA

tundra

First published by Doubleday Canada, 2005
Published in this edition by Tundra Books, 2022

Tundra Books, an imprint of Penguin Random House Canada Young Readers,
a division of Penguin Random House of Canada Limited

Library and Archives Canada Cataloguing in Publication

Title: Swimming in the monsoon sea / Shyam Selvadurai.
Names: Selvadurai, Shyam, 1965- author.
Description: Originally published: 2005.
Identifiers: Canadiana 20210363711 | ISBN 9781774880333 (softcover)
Classification: LCC PS8587.E445 S95 2022 | DDC jC813/.54—dc23

Published simultaneously in the United States of America by
Tundra Books of Northern New York, an imprint of
Penguin Random House Canada Young Readers,
a division of Penguin Random House of Canada Limited

Library of Congress Control Number: 2004117239

Designed by Sophie Paas-Lang
The text was set in Adobe Garamond

Printed in the U.S.A.

www.penguinrandomhouse.ca

1st Printing

Penguin
Random House
TUNDRA BOOKS

*This novel, though fictional, is filled with details from my happy childhood in Sri Lanka: as a way to enshrine that time, and to, perhaps, bid it good-bye.*

*I dedicate this book, with great love, to those wonderful companions of my youth: my brother, Tino, and my sisters, Pnina and Revathy.*

"But people can't, unhappily, invent their mooring posts, their lovers and their friends, anymore than they can invent their parents. Life gives these and also takes them away and the great difficulty is to say Yes to life."

From *Giovanni's Room* by James Baldwin

# Sri Lanka

≈≈≈

1980

# I

# The Silent Mynah

~~~~~~~~~~~~~
~~~~~~~~~~~~~

Amrith, reaching the top step to the terrace, paused for a moment and looked out over the rooftops toward the sea, visible through the palm fronds of coconut trees in the various gardens between his house and the beach. In the dawn light, bands of silver were appearing on the crests of the waves, as if a giant louver in the sky was opening up, one slat at a time. A breeze was coming up from the ocean, bringing a saltiness to his lips. Amrith could usually tell, by the sound of the waves against the sand, whether the tide was in or out. But this was a monsoon sea, wild and savage, and it had eaten up the beach. Even at low tide, the waves still crashed against the rocks that held them back from eroding the land.

The birds in the aviary had noticed Amrith's presence and, as he crossed the terrace, the budgerigars twittered in anticipation of the food he might be bringing them. There had been a monsoon storm last night, and Amrith had to walk around large puddles to reach the aviary. Once he had let himself into the safety porch, he secured the door behind him and looked around.

The storm had not caused any damage to the aviary. A few feeding cups had been knocked over by the wind, their seed scattered on the ground, and a perch broken. These were minor destructions, considering the fierceness of the storm. Kuveni, the mynah, was already in the shelter part of the aviary, where the food and water were kept. She was flapping her wings and making little darts in the direction of the hexagonal flight area to keep the budgerigars away so she would have first rights to whatever food Amrith was bringing. Kuveni, named after the mythical demoness of Sri Lankan lore, was vicious and spiteful and bossy, and not really suitable for colony breeding. Yet Amrith could not bring himself to isolate her. He liked her spunk, her bossiness. He just wished that she would talk. He had been trying for the last four months, since she was brought to him, to try and get her to say his name, but she remained mute. Now, he stood back, holding out the halved papaw he had brought and repeating, "Amrith, Amrith," over and over again, hoping that, by tantalizing her, she would speak out of desperation or annoyance. Yet she said nothing, and only beat her wings against the mesh that separated them.

With a sigh, he let himself in. The moment he put the papaw down on a ledge, Kuveni flew to it and began to devour the pulp.

Until Kuveni had been given to him, Amrith had not realized how beautiful mynahs were. Here in Colombo, they were common as crows and he had not paid them the slightest attention. Being this close to one, however, had made him see how exquisite they were – their silky black heads; their warm brown plumage; the golden yellow of their throats, upper breasts, bills, and feet; the snowy white tips of their tails.

Voices in the side garden below distracted Amrith from his contemplation. Aunty Bundle and her old ayah, Jane-Nona, were discussing the damage caused to the living room roof by the storm last night. Some of the tiles had blown away, leaving a gaping hole. Roofers were very busy during the monsoon period, and the women were worried that, if the hole was not repaired in time, they would have to cancel the big birthday party for Aunty Bundle's daughters, which was to take place next month.

The women had finished their conversation and Aunty Bundle started up the stairs that led to the terrace. As her footsteps drew near, a black mood, which Amrith had managed to hold at bay, swept over him like a wave, carrying him out to a darkness he did not want to face.

"Amrith?"

Aunty Bundle stood on the top step, looking towards him in the aviary. Her plump face, usually merry, was sober and stark without any makeup, and her eyes, which always sparkled with laughter, were dull and red from crying. Instead of her regular bright sarong and crisp lace blouse, she wore the plain white sari of mourning. The jeweled peacock that hung from a chain around her waist was gone, as were her gold bangles. The only jewelry she wore was her gold cross on a chain.

Amrith felt a sharp anger take hold as he looked at her through the mesh. Why did she insist on dressing in clothes of mourning every year on this day? It had been eight years since his mother's death and yet, from Aunty Bundle's clothes, one would think it was the day of the funeral itself. He wanted to yell that it was all too ridiculous – this remembering, this anniversary. He was sick of it, sick of the whole thing. Today was the first day of his holidays. It was unfair, utterly unfair, that he had to get up so early and go to Mass and then the graveyard. He should have been allowed to sleep in.

"Son," Aunty Bundle said, taking a step forward, "it's time to go."

"*Um*, yes, Aunty," he replied politely. "I'll come in a moment."

She nodded and went back down the terrace steps.

The moment she was gone, Amrith leaned against the mesh and closed his eyes. He thought of how, on the first anniversary of his mother's death, he had rebelled against going to church and the graveyard. He wished that he was seven again and not fourteen – that he could once again throw a tantrum and refuse to go. On that first anniversary, he had lain on the floor and screamed when Aunty Bundle tried to make him put on his church clothes. Finally her husband, Uncle Lucky, had intervened. Though Amrith, by then, loved and trusted Uncle Lucky more than anyone else in the world, he was still afraid of him. Uncle Lucky would not let him get away with anything. And so, while Uncle Lucky had stood over him sternly, he had hiccuped and sobbed, but got dressed. When he was done, Uncle Lucky had sat on the edge of the bed and made Amrith stand between his thighs, while he combed his hair. As he did so, he had spoken to him gravely, telling Amrith he must never forget his mother; that the past was very important as, from time to time, we could call on it to help us. And if we did not know our past, then we could not call on it.

Kuveni had sated herself on papaw and she was perched on a swing, looking at Amrith, her head to one side. His anger flowed towards her. "You're useless," he said softly, his eyes narrowed. "I should just release you into the garden and get another mynah that will talk."

The car was starting up downstairs in the garage. Amrith left the aviary, closing the door behind him and checking the lock twice.

The aviary was a gift from Aunty Bundle, for Amrith's thirteenth birthday last year. Her close friend and colleague, the famous architect Lucien Lindamulagé, had a giant aviary in his back garden; he was almost as passionate about his birds as he was about his buildings. Amrith, from the time he was little, would spend hours in the old man's aviary. Aunty Bundle consulted Lucien Lindamulagé on the building of the aviary. She did not allow Uncle Lucky to contribute a cent. It was to be solely her gift. She told Amrith and her two daughters, Selvi and Mala, that construction was going on to turn the terrace into a properly

landscaped roof-garden and that they were forbidden to go
up there. Then, on Amrith's birthday, when he came home
from school, Aunty Bundle had taken him by the hand and
hurried him through the side garden and up the terrace
stairs. He had gasped when he saw the aviary, all the
budgerigars twittering and flying around at the sight of
humans, whom they associated with food.

As Amrith went down the terrace stairs, he thought of
how Aunty Bundle's generosity always made him feel uneasy.
He felt that what she did for him, she did out of guilt. Aunty
Bundle blamed herself, to this day, for his mother's death.

~~~~~
~~~~~

Usually, when Amrith went to church, it was on Sunday for
late-morning Mass. The church would be flooded with
sunlight through the dome above the altar and the side
windows. The various murals – Saint Sebastian, his head
lifted in rapture to the heavens, his scantily clad body
pierced with a hundred arrows; Mary Magdalene kneeling
before Christ, wiping His feet with the veil of her hair;
benevolent Saint Anthony – would be clearly visible.

Though Amrith found the Sunday Mass boring, Aunty
Bundle's daughters, Selvi and Mala, were present, and so
they ended up having a good time. Selvi, who was plump,
pretty, and vivacious like her mother, was frequently in
scrapes for being a tomboy. Her goal during Mass was to
make Amrith and Mala laugh. When Father Anthony

would say, "Let us stand and bow our heads to receive the word of God, Our Heavenly Father," Selvi would lean over and whisper "goad," which was the way the priest pronounced "God." This would set Amrith off with a snuffle of laughter. Then she would add in a sibilant whisper, "Amrith, Amrith, Amrith, look at Father Anthony's hair. It's like an Afro, *nah.*" Amrith's shoulders would shake uncontrollably and, to push him completely over the edge, Selvi would give a soft wolf-whistle and say, "*Hoo-hoo,* sexy-sexy Disco-Father." Amrith would almost weep with silent laughter, begging her in a whisper, "Shut up, men, please shut up."

Even Mala, who had recently become very religious (and who participated in the Mass with fervor, her hands clasped tightly to her chest), would lose her devout expression and start to giggle, which was the ultimate triumph for Selvi.

This Monday morning, however, the church was almost empty. The scattering of worshippers had gathered in the front pews, as the lights and ceiling fans in the rest of the church had been turned off to save electricity. They appeared huddled against the gloom of the church behind them. The darkness of his surroundings seemed to enter Amrith's very soul as he automatically stood and sat through the recitation of the Mass. To his right, just beyond the pew, was a statue of Our Lady, her arms held out in a gesture of welcome as if beckoning the supplicant to her, the smile on her face gentle and loving. As Amrith gazed at her, his mind, over which he kept such rigid control when it came to the past, slipped silently away from him, and he was back on that tea estate where he had spent the first six years of his life.

He was coming home from school, so longing to see his mother after their morning separation. He ran through the massive iron gates into the graveled front compound of the estate bungalow and around the side of the house to the back, where a veranda flanked the rear of the house. There, as always, he found his mother. He loved that moment when he turned the corner, dashed up the veranda steps, and saw her sitting in her chair wearing a cream cardigan and cotton trousers. A magenta batik scarf, folded into an Alice band, kept back the frizzy exuberance of her hair. When she held her arms out to him, the bangles on her wrists would tinkle in welcome. He would run to her, snuggling into that familiar smell of eau de cologne.

She always sat in the same cane chair, which had a back shaped like a fanned-out peacock tail. If she was not there when he ran up onto the veranda, he would bury his face in the cushion, breathing in her eau de cologne, not lifting his head until she had come back out to him.

He was six years old by then and he knew that, compared to the fair-skinned, plump female stars of Sinhala and Tamil films, his mother was not considered conventionally beautiful. Her skin was too dark; she was too thin, too awkwardly long-limbed. But he loved her eyes and the way she would look at him mischievously from under her long lashes when they were playing; the way her frizzy hair would burst out all over her face when she released it from her Alice band. She was, in her own way, beautiful.

Later, after she had fed him his lunch, he would take his afternoon rest on a daybed on the veranda. His mother took her rest on another daybed, a little away from him. He had learnt to judge his mother's mood by what she did during that time. If she was at ease, she would invite him to lie with her, while she read her *Femina* magazines, one arm around him as he cuddled up against her side.

If his mother was in a low mood, however, she would lie by herself or, most often, go through the French windows into the drawing room. After a moment, Amrith would hear a scratching and hissing before the music started. She played the same two records over and over again: Pat Boone and Nat King Cole, records from her youth. Above the sound of the songs, he would hear her pacing. Sometimes, she strode out onto the veranda, as if she was going somewhere. But when she got to the edge, she stood, her right arm over her stomach, her hand clutching her left elbow. She would stand like that for a long time, occasionally brushing her palm across her cheeks.

Amrith knew the cause of her sorrow. It was his father.

This man was a stranger to Amrith. He had never actually seen him. His father was gone from the house by the time Amrith awoke; his lunch was sent to the office in a tiffin carrier; he had dinner at the club. On Sundays his father stayed home, and then Amrith remained with his ayah, Selamma, in the tea workers' quarters, until his father left for the club at five. Amrith only knew his father as a sound, a voice shouting in the night.

When he knelt beside his bed to pray each evening, he would repeat the last line of his prayer over and over again as if it was a mantra that would bring peace that night, a mantra that would stop his father's raging.

When the night sounds did occur, Amrith would sit up in bed, his knees drawn to his chest, his eyes squeezed tight, trying to persuade himself that his father's shouts were actually sneezes, that the rising inflection of his mother's voice was tinkling laughter as she tickled his father's nose with a feather; that their dog, Bhootaya, was baying outside the front door because she had been left out of the fun.

Later, when Amrith was half-asleep, he would feel his bed heave as his mother got in beside him. She would curl around him, her hand slipping into his. The smell of sweat on her was sharp like the Singer oil she used on her sewing machine. Her body would be trembling from trying not to cry.

"Amrith, child."

He came to himself, to find Aunty Bundle holding out her handkerchief to him. He stared at it for a moment, puzzled, then he felt the wetness on his cheeks. He took the handkerchief, hurriedly turned away, and wiped his face. When he handed it back, he avoided her sympathetic gaze. His anger towards her returned sharply.

~~~~~
~~~~~

The graveyard, where his mother was buried, was in the center of Colombo. Its many acres were divided into different sections for the various religions of Sri Lanka. One part of the graveyard was taken up with crematoriums for the Buddhists and Hindus, who did not bury their dead but rather cremated the bodies and scattered the ashes in the sea or in rivers. The Muslims had their area, as did the numerous Christian sects.

Aunty Bundle's driver, Mendis, parked the car outside the gate that led into the Christian section, and she and Amrith got out.

There were hawkers in front of the gates selling bunches of flowers, marigold garlands, lotuses, and sticks of incense from their stalls. Aunty Bundle stopped at one of them to buy two bouquets of flowers. She handed one to Amrith and, as he took it, he smelt the sharp odor of carnations, a smell he always associated with death and funerals.

They entered through the gates and made their way among the graves, towards the place where his mother was buried. They were passing through a section of the cemetery that, during the time of colonialism, when the British ruled Sri Lanka, had been White Only. The British had buried their dead in this separate area, apart from the Sri Lankans. It was in a dilapidated state, as the descendants of these dead colonizers were no longer around to keep their ancestors' graves up. The few tombstones that were still standing were so covered in moss, it was impossible to read the engravings. Most of the stones, however, had disintegrated under the tropical heat and humidity. Just fragments lay in the tall grass, with surnames like *Smith, Barclay, Woodson* – names that had once belonged to someone's father or mother or child or sibling. Another fragment had the words *Dearly Beloved,* with an engraving of roses around it. Another fragment, just the word *Mother.* As they made their way through the knee-high grass, Amrith was sure that they were stepping on graves.

When they reached his mother's grave, the grass and weeds were high on the mound. The flowers Aunty Bundle had laid, when she visited a month ago, were withered and crisped brown. There had been a recent burial in the adjoining plot, the date of death on the tombstone reading *July 1980.* Clods of soil were scattered on his mother's grave.

*"Ttttch."* Aunty Bundle clicked her tongue against the back of her teeth in annoyance. "I pay that cemetery keeper, and see, nothing has been done."

She knelt down and began to pull at the weeds and grass. Amrith did not help her. He stood there, his face averted from the grave, wishing that this whole ordeal would end.

Once Aunty Bundle was satisfied with the state of the grave, she indicated for him to kneel beside her and together they said a decade of the rosary. When they were done, Amrith got to his feet and dusted the knees of his white trousers, which were stained with soil.

"Amrith?"

He looked up to see Aunty Bundle regarding him with a mixture of worry and hope. Even before she spoke, he knew what she was going to say. She asked him the same questions every year.

"Son, don't you remember your mother at all?"

He shook his head.

"You don't remember that time, when I visited you at the estate?"

He shook his head again and avoided looking at her.

Later, as they were walking back towards the gate, Amrith kept a few steps behind Aunty Bundle. He felt a curious bitter pleasure in denying her his memories.

## 2

# Aunty Bundle

~~~~~~~~~
~~~~~~~~~

And yet Amrith's mind, his traitorous mind, as if rebelling against such meanness towards Aunty Bundle, came in and swept him away to the memory of the first time he had heard her name.

He had returned one morning from school to find his mother seated in her usual cane chair, her hands clasped behind her head, looking out at the distant mountains.

"Amrith." She lowered her arms and turned to him. "I received a letter today, darling. From an old friend in Colombo." Picking up a sheet of thin blue paper, she beckoned him forward.

He peered at the letter, unable to decipher the exuberant scrawl. His mother smiled faintly. "My friend always had the most horrible hand." She began to read the letter.

*"My dear Asha,*

*I am an interior decorator now and work with the well-known architect Lucien Lindamulagé. We are renovating an old estate bungalow into a hotel, not far from where you live. It would be nice to catch up and reminisce about the good old days. I do hope you still remember them. As for me, I have never forgotten. I will be staying at the local rest house and I will wait for you to telephone me before I visit.*

*Love*
*Bundle"*

Amrith was surprised by the formality of the letter. It was unheard of for someone, particularly an old friend, to wait on a telephone invitation to visit. When people visited, they never called or made an appointment, but usually dropped in casually, unannounced. Then there was her name, the oddity of it. Bundle. Like a bundle of firewood, or a bundle of papers.

"Ammi, why does she have such a strange name?"

"Her real name is Beatrice," his mother said with a smile, "but she was such a happy baby that her parents called her Bundle-of-Joy and then just Bundle."

"She sounds like a really jolly person, Ammi. Are you going to phone her?"

His mother folded up the letter. She picked up his plate of rice and curry, which was lying under a fly-cover on the table, and began to divide it into mouthfuls with her right hand. "Amrith, you are a big boy now, six years old and everything. So there are things I can tell you, things you must understand. Your father . . . he's a very jealous man. He does not like people visiting me. He does not like it at all. Soon after we married, I . . . I broke off contact with Aunty Bundle to please him, even though she was my oldest and dearest friend. Why, Bundle and I were like sisters back then. Our families lived next door to each other and we grew up together. We were inseparable all through –" She gazed into the distance. Her eyes were like those dark wet stones he picked up out of streams.

Amrith pulled at her sleeve to distract her from her sorrow. "When you were girls, Ammi, what was your favorite thing to do?"

She thought about his question for a moment. "Our best times together were when we went on vacation to Sanasuma, my family's holiday home." She smiled, lost in a memory. "My, what glorious adventures Bundle and I had there. We would pack a picnic lunch and go for long treks up the mountains. When we got too hot, we would put on our bathing suits and swim in some little stream that we had discovered. Sometimes when we were picnicking in a field, deer would come to graze. It was magical. Everything about Sanasuma was magical. The house was perched on a plateau surrounded by mountains. You could see for miles and miles down below. And, right by Sanasuma, a stream made its way down the hillside, forming a waterfall at one point and tumbling into a rock pool at another. We would spend hours in that rock pool."

"I would love to see Sanasuma, Ammi."

His mother sighed. "Maybe one day, son. Maybe one day."

She offered him a mouthful of food.

~~~~~

Amrith might never have met Aunty Bundle, and his whole life might have been different, if his father had not been called away unexpectedly to Colombo for meetings with the National Tea Board. He would be gone a week.

Amrith heard the good news from his ayah, Selamma, when she came to pick him up after school. He felt an incredible happiness take hold of him and, when he got home, he ran around the side of the house and found his mother waiting for him by the veranda steps, a look of equal joy on her face.

"Amrith!" She picked him up, twirled him around, and set him down. "I have a surprise for you." She grabbed his hand and led him past the veranda.

Their garden had a narrow shelf of grass from which the land sloped down sharply to the lawn below. In the center of the lawn, Amrith saw that a picnic lunch had been laid out on a mat.

When they got down the steps that were carved into the slope, Amrith was delighted that, instead of boring rice and curry, they were having boiled eggs, ham sandwiches, lemonade, and – he could hardly believe it – chips.

Once they had finished their lunch, his mother said to him, "Son, what else shall we do, now that, you know, we're alone?"

"What *shall* we do?" He lay with his head in her lap. "What would you like to do, Ammi?"

She looked down at him and then away. He knew what she was thinking.

"You should invite her, Ammi. I would really like to meet Aunty Bundle."

"I don't know, son, I just don't know."

Yet, when he came home the next afternoon, there was a car in the driveway. He ran towards the house, around the corner, and up the veranda steps.

And there she was, Aunty Bundle, alone, seated in his mother's chair. She was facing away from him, practically hidden by the intricate canework that made up the design of the peacock tail. All that was clearly visible were the ornate leather Indian slippers on her feet, a silver chain around one chubby ankle.

She made a slight movement, but did not turn around.

Amrith walked behind the visitor and went to stand by the cane chair on the other side of the table. Across from him was a beautiful woman. She was wearing a blouse of fine white cotton, with lacework on the front and puffed sleeves that ended at her dimpled elbows. Her skirt was an ankle-length sarong of shimmering turquoise, with a thick gold band down the front. Around her plump waist was a delicate and finely filigreed chain-belt. From its clasp, a length of chain hung down her hip, a jeweled peacock at the end. A gold cross on a chain nestled in the indentation of her bosom. Amrith's gaze traveled up to the woman's face. He had already learnt from his mother that her friend was half-Dutch Burgher, half-Sinhalese, and so he was not surprised by her light complexion, like milk-tea. She had a heart-shaped dimply face, a turned-up nose, and caramel eyes. Her hair rose out of a widow's peak and was back-combed.

Aunty Bundle was regarding him too, her head slightly to one side, her eyes brilliant. "Amrith, dear," she said, holding out her hand, "I have waited so long to meet you, thought so very much about you."

He found himself going to her. It was her voice that drew him, its low murmur like a stream running over pebbles. She put an arm around him and drew him to her. There was a deftness to her touch. She held him but did not confine him in any way. Amrith allowed himself to sink into her, let her stroke his head. Her perfume was sweet but also woody, like freshly cut logs. Bhootaya, their dog, who never trusted strangers, was lying by Aunty Bundle's chair, her snout on her paws.

His mother came out onto the veranda. She smiled at him as if to say, "Here is the thing you wanted."

He went and hugged her.

"Now, Asha." Aunty Bundle stood up, a sudden liveliness entering her voice, her eyes. "Remember, you promised me a tour of the garden."

"Yes-yes." His mother's face lit up with a girlish vivacity Amrith had never seen before.

The two women went down the veranda steps, their arms linked. Whatever awkwardness there had been over his mother's breaking off contact, all those years ago, had been dealt with before Amrith got home.

When Aunty Bundle was at the top of the slope, looking down to the garden, she cried out, "Ash-a! My, how lovely! The roses, goodness me, I have never seen such a profusion." She held her arms out to encompass the large roses, riotous on the bushes below, in various shades and colors from golden orange to delicate pink to feathery white to velvety red.

"Did you do all this yourself?" Aunty Bundle said, turning to his mother.

She nodded, delighted at her friend's wonder at the roses, for which she had a great passion.

"But what talent, Asha, what a marvel!" Aunty Bundle pressed his mother's arm. "Come-come, I must have a closer look at your talent, *nah*."

His mother glowed from the praise. "There are steps over there to the –"

"Steps?" Aunty Bundle cried, with a grin. "*Ttttch,* you may be an old woman but not me, miss." She had been carrying a white parasol, which she now snapped shut and tucked under her arm. She hitched up her sarong to her knees and kicked off her slippers. "Last one down has to be servant-for-the-day. Come on, Amrith! Now. Ready –" His mother grinned and kicked off her slippers. Amrith took his position on one knee. "– Steady go!"

They raced down the hill, the women squealing, their arms flailing at their sides like birds that could not fly. Amrith gritted his teeth and beat them both.

When they reached the bottom, the women plopped down on the grass, laughing. Then Aunty Bundle rose to her feet, snapped her parasol open, and the two of them began a tour of the garden. Amrith sat a little way up the slope, hugging his knees to his chest, watching his mother's friend.

He was enchanted with Aunty Bundle. She had brought such immediate happiness. He had never known that his mother's face could light up in such a way. Amrith could tell, from Aunty Bundle's jeweled peacock, fine clothes, heavy gold bangles, and silk parasol, that she was much richer than they were. Yet, there was nothing stiff about her at all and, in fact, he felt he had known her for a long time.

Aunty Bundle stayed for lunch. Later, while Amrith lay on his daybed, the two women had tea and Aunty Bundle talked of her life in Colombo.

Amrith, listening to their conversation, learnt that Aunty Bundle was married to a man named Lucky (short for Lukshman), whom his mother seemed to know as well, from her earlier life in Colombo. This Lucky, or Uncle Lucky, as Amrith would soon come to call him, was very rich and owned a company called Ceylon Aquariums, which exported exotic fish all over the world. They had a daughter named Mala, whom Aunty Bundle referred to with a fond smile as "a little grandmother," and another daughter named Selvi, who Aunty Bundle said, with a twinkle in her eye, was "a devilish handful."

The world Aunty Bundle spoke of – her family; her house that had been designed by the architect Lucien Lindamulagé and was a good example of something called precolonial architecture; her old ayah, Jane-Nona; her dogs, Eva, Zsa Zsa, and Magda, who were such ugly mongrels that Aunty Bundle, out of pity, had named them after three beautiful Hollywood sisters – all this had seemed so distant, so foreign from Amrith's own life.

Lying there on his daybed, listening intently with his mouth agape, he could not have imagined how soon he would be a part of that world; how soon he would become a member of the Manuel-Pillai family.

# 3

# Ceylon Aquariums

~~~~~
~~~~~

Aunty Bundle had a design meeting that morning with Lucien Lindamulagé for a new project they were working on. She dropped Amrith outside the gates of their house and left immediately.

The compound in which the Manuel-Pillai home stood had a tall parapet wall all around it. The gates opened into an extensive cobbled front courtyard, with a large jak tree growing in the center. The house was at the far end of the courtyard. Double doors led into the living room. It had no rear wall and opened directly onto the back garden, the black-and-white checked tile flooring giving way to squares of dark and light gravel on the patio. There were accordion doors that could be drawn across to cut off the garden during a rainstorm, or at night. To the right of the living room, on a slightly raised level, was the dining room. Two steps led up to it. From the dining room, swinging doors

provided an entrance to the pantry and kitchen. To the left
of the living room was an antechamber, called the library
because of the bookshelves in it. This library had two doors
at either end, one leading to the girls' room and the other to
Uncle Lucky and Aunty Bundle's room. Their bedrooms
had French windows that opened into a walled side garden.
Amrith's room was slightly separate from the rest of the
house and was reached by a door in what seemed the left
boundary wall of the courtyard, but, instead, surprisingly,
opened into his bedroom, from which French windows also
led to the walled side garden.

Once Amrith had showered and changed, he went across
the front courtyard and into the living room. There was a
large barrel now under the hole in the roof to catch rain that
fell through. He made his way past the barrel to the dining
room and then through to the kitchen. Jane-Nona had kept
his breakfast under a fly-cover in the pantry. Amrith
perched on a tall stool and munched on his cold scrambled
eggs and toast, staring out at the kitchen garden. The light
that came in through the window puddled and rippled on
the fridge and spice cupboard. Selvi and Mala had left for
their various activities a while ago, and a quiet reigned
throughout the house, broken only by Jane-Nona pounding
something in the mortar – a rhythmic *thump-thump* –
followed by the scraping of a metal spoon against stone,
before the process was repeated. His holiday stretched
before him with nothing to do and a gloom settled over
him like a heavy cape.

The school year, which began in January, was divided into three semesters, separated from one another by month-long holidays in April, August, and December. Of all the holidays, August was the dullest. In April, the hottest month of the year, Amrith and the Manuel-Pillais, like almost everyone else in their social circle, escaped to the chalets and cottages of the cool hill country. In December, there was the excitement of Christmas, with its endless rounds of dinners and social visits. In August, however, there were no such distractions. This vacation was going to be particularly tedious because, due to his and the girls' schools being used as exam centers, their holiday would stretch to six weeks.

Amrith sighed. Already, more than half of 1980 was over and, despite his hopes that this first year of the new decade would bring exciting changes to his life, there had been none. Things went on in their boring way. At four-teen, it often seemed to him that his life was already set, with nothing much to look forward to.

Once he had dawdled over his breakfast, Amrith went to stand at the gate, peering down the deserted road, as if he expected something to materialize beyond the shimmering tar. A group of neighborhood boys came out of a house, on their way to a field nearby. They were carrying cricket bats, wickets, fielding gloves, and a ball. Their voices were raised in gruff competition and two of them were scuffling. Amrith hurried back inside, not wanting them to see him.

In the courtyard, Eva, Zsa Zsa, and Magda had gathered around the jak tree, their snouts twitching upwards as they

listened to a squirrel scampering through the branches.
Recently, a squirrel had missed its footing and fallen. Eva
had captured it in her jaws, but Zsa Zsa and Magda had
fought her for it, tearing bits of the live squirrel from her
mouth. They saw Amrith and came rushing over, their tails
manic metronomes. He waved them off. "*Shoo*, get away,
you disgusting old things." They crept back to the tree, hurt.

"Amrith?"

The door to the master bedroom was ajar. Uncle Lucky
was knotting his tie in front of the full-length mirror on the
almirah door. Without turning around, he crooked his
finger at Amrith, who went and stood by the almirah.

Uncle Lucky was tall and lean and very dark-skinned.
He had angular features that were set in a customarily
severe expression – an effect heightened by the fact that his
heavy-lidded eyes were magnified by his square, black,
plastic-framed glasses. All his family and staff, however,
were quite aware of the person behind this facade. Uncle
Lucky, though he was always accusing his wife of being
gullible to any hard-luck story, was far easier to touch up for
money and favors than Aunty Bundle.

"Amrith," Uncle Lucky said, frowning down at him,
"isn't there any boy from your drama society you'd like to
have come and spend the day?"

Amrith felt the heat rising in his neck. There wasn't.
Though he was respected for his acting talent, at the same
time, none of the boys had ever made overtures of friend-
ship towards him.

Uncle Lucky cocked his foot on a cane side chair and began to retie his shoelaces. "This won't do, Amrith." He lowered his foot with a snap and stood, legs apart. "The other day I was at the Inter-Continental Hotel, waiting to meet a client, when I got chatting with this foreigner from an American organization that is setting up skills-training centers in poor areas. I asked him, 'Sir, what do you think is the most important skill a young man should have for his future life?' Do you know what he answered? 'Typing.' Typing! Evidently, in ten years, computers will be running everything. Not knowing how to type will be like not knowing how to add. Can you imagine? And people here think typing is infra dig, just for clerks and steno-girls. So," Uncle Lucky picked up a stack of files, "this holiday, I want you to come every morning and study typing at my office."

It was not a request, and Amrith felt relieved.

Uncle Lucky held up his hand. "Five minutes. Run and put on something nice. I don't want you coming like a beggar. No Bata slippers, please."

When he came out to the car, Uncle Lucky was already seated in the back. His driver, Soma, smiled companionably as Amrith got into the front seat beside him.

Uncle Lucky's aquarium was in the town of Negambo because it was close to the airport and also by the sea. Amrith and the girls had been there many times. The fish tanks were housed on four open corridors that formed a rectangle around a courtyard. This allowed for a maximum amount of sunlight, and the circulation of air.

Uncle Lucky's office, however, was in Colombo's Fort, on historic Chatham Street, with its colonial buildings from the last century – whitewashed facades with pillars and arches and colonnaded arcades.

When they went shopping in Fort, Aunty Bundle often brought them by the office. Uncle Lucky would take them to Pagoda for pastries or, if times were particularly good for him, to the Grand Oriental Hotel, for lunch in the Rainbow Room overlooking the harbor.

Once Soma had dropped them and gone to park, Amrith looked up and down Chatham Street. Things were very much the same – still the crush of pedestrians jostling by, the street hawkers selling everything from mothballs and combs to cheap Chinese leather goods and windup toys; the cacophony of horns and cars backfiring, the hot oily smell of diesel fumes.

The broad stairs, which led up to Uncle Lucky's office on the second floor, were in need of polishing, the intricate Moorish tiling of the foyer cracked and chipped. After the street, there was a stately silence, a coolness. Their footsteps echoed as they went up the broad stairs.

A panel fronted the landing of the second floor. Its bottom half was golden brown wood; the top half, frosted glass. A door in the panel led to Uncle Lucky's office. A gold plate on the door carried the inscription, *Ceylon Aquariums,* in large curving letters, and below it the name of the proprietor, *Lukshman Manuel-Pillai.*

They entered into the lively sound of typewriters and chatter, the clinking of teacups against saucers. Uncle Lucky's presence did not bring silence, rather it was as if someone had turned down the volume on a radio. As Amrith followed Uncle Lucky towards his cubicle – the only one in the office – he looked around, nodding and smiling shyly to the familiar faces.

There were four workers in all. The steno-girls, Mangalika and Susanthika, wore flowered frocks and had waist-length hair, which they wore in a plait. Mr. Balasunderam, the accountant, was rapidly losing his hair, but had chosen not to go gracefully into baldness. He grew out the sides and pasted the graying strands across his bald head. Amrith and the girls were fond of him – when they were younger, he always had Delta Toffees for them – but it made them giggle to watch those strands gradually slip off the top of his head and plop down onto his shoulders.

Miss Rani was the office manager. She wore bright nylon saris that rustled like plastic sheeting when she moved about. Her hair was parted in the center and tied in a bun at the back. Being deeply devout, she always had a vermilion stain at the front of her parting and a dusting of white ash on her forehead, from having gone to the temple in the morning. Miss Rani carried a handkerchief tucked into the strap of her wristwatch, which she used to delicately wipe the sweat off her upper lip and temples. There was a burnt smell to her of synthetic fabric that had been ironed at a too-high temperature. She was from the Tamil capital of Jaffna, in the north of Sri Lanka.

Uncle Lucky's relationship with Miss Rani was different from that with any of his other workers. He had a certain reverence towards her, yet, at the same time, a brotherly interest in her welfare. He paid for any business courses she wanted to take and was always terribly proud of her achievements. If he needed advice, he talked to Miss Rani.

Once Uncle Lucky was seated in his office, he called on Miss Rani to take over Amrith. She installed him at an old typewriter in the corner, put a book of typing exercises in front of him, and showed him how to keep his hands on the keys, his wrists curved upwards. As Miss Rani bent over him to demonstrate the first exercise – *ff jj ff jj dd kk dd kk ss ll ss ll aa ;; aa ;;* – he looked at her and wondered, as he often had, about the nature of her relationship with Uncle Lucky. Amrith was sure she was not his mistress because Uncle Lucky adored his wife and considered men who had mistresses to be cads. Also, Aunty Bundle heartily approved of his generosity towards Miss Rani. (And besides, Amrith could not imagine Miss Rani, with the ash on her forehead, being anyone's mistress.) It was Uncle Lucky's peculiar reverence for her, as if Miss Rani was a treasure that he had discovered by accident and looked after with great care, that puzzled Amrith.

Miss Rani came by occasionally to offer words of encouragement and to correct his errors. The precision and effort it took to gain command over his fingers was so absorbing that Amrith was surprised when there was a stirring amongst the staff, the clang of tiffin carriers being opened up, the smell of rice and curry in the air. He had really enjoyed his time in this cool high-ceilinged office with its hum of activity; really enjoyed the challenge of mastering the typing exercises.

When they were standing on Chatham Street, waiting for Soma to bring the car around, Amrith glanced at Uncle Lucky and felt a great love for this man, who had always looked out for his interests.

During that terrible time of his mother's funeral, Uncle Lucky had stood behind him like a rock, while Aunty Bundle, in her grief and guilt, had fallen to pieces. It was Uncle Lucky who had told him how his parents had died – the awful and mysterious circumstances surrounding their death. But, before Uncle Lucky had done so, he had put his hands on Amrith's shoulders, looked him keenly in the eyes, and said, "I want to make you a promise, son. You will never, ever, be a stranger in my house."

# 4

# The Barrier of the Past

~~~~~~~~~
~~~~~~~~~

Amrith's black mood returned with greater ferocity that afternoon, from having been held in abeyance for a few hours at Uncle Lucky's office.

Storm clouds had been gathering all through lunch and, finally, just when the family began their afternoon rest, there was a crash of thunder, a burst of lightning, and the rain poured down from the skies without any preliminary drizzle (as it often did during a monsoon). Amrith lay on his bed, his hands cupping the back of his neck, his room darkened by the torrent outside. He felt that familiar inner blackness come in and sweep him out, like a current. Once again, he was helpless against its power – like being held underwater in the salty murkiness of a churned-up sea.

These black moods were quite recent and they frightened him. They had started about a year ago, around the time he turned thirteen. With his changing body, it seemed that a change had occurred within. When he thought of himself before he was thirteen, it was as a dashing-about child, with no thoughts distinct from the dictates and actions of his body. As he passed into his teenage years, his mind seemed to separate more and more from his body, causing him to see himself from a distance. And this detachment, paradoxically, had brought a great flooding of emotions. In the past, his sense of sadness over the loss of his mother had been confined, for the most part, to her death anniversary and, perhaps, a little at Christmas. But now he felt dejected quite often. Her absence made him aware that he had no real family. His relatives on both his father's and mother's sides wanted nothing to do with him. His parents had married against the wishes of their families and they had eloped to do so. The child of such a marriage was often rejected by his relatives.

Amrith sat up in bed and drew his legs to his chest. As he rested his chin on his knees, a memory arose of a visit two women had paid Aunty Bundle a few months ago.

They were old school friends. One of them lived in Colombo and kept in touch with Aunty Bundle occasionally. The other had just come back from Australia to settle in Sri Lanka. She had been living abroad for the past ten years with her daughters.

Amrith had immediately disliked the woman from Australia and he could tell that Aunty Bundle was less than delighted to see her again. She was a hawkish-looking woman, with a beak of a nose and closely set eyes. Amrith

was the only other family member home and, since he
and the girls were expected to greet visitors, he had gone
out to the courtyard where the women were seated with
Aunty Bundle.

The moment the woman from Australia saw him, she
cried out, "But, Bundle, who is this boy? I didn't know you
had a son."

The other school friend looked disconcerted. She had
clearly told this woman exactly who he was. Warned her,
Amrith could not help feeling.

Aunty Bundle had also seen through the woman's
charade and her voice was icy as she introduced Amrith –
the son of her friend Asha, grandson of the late QC
Fonseka, the famous lawyer.

"*Aah*, he is just visiting you, then," the woman from
Australia said disingenuously.

"No," Aunty Bundle replied, with even greater coldness, "Amrith is our son now."

In all the years Amrith had lived here, there had never
been a need to explain his presence. In Sri Lankan society,
all such personal information was secretly passed between
people to prevent socially awkward situations from arising.

Amrith, having done his social duty, was free to leave,
and he went across the courtyard to his bedroom. He did
not know why but, once he was in his room, he left his door
slightly ajar and stood by it, listening.

After a while, Aunty Bundle went inside to answer a
phone call. The moment she left, the other school friend

said to the woman from Australia, "What on earth, Ratna? I already told you about the boy, *nah*."

"Yes-yes," Ratna replied, "but I just wanted to make my point clear."

"Which is?"

"That I have brought my teenage daughters back to this country to ensure they meet the right sorts of people, rather than those savage Australians. And I didn't go through all the trouble of relocating to have them mix with the likes of that boy."

"But why? He is, after all, the grandson of QC Fonseka, a fine family."

"Yes, but his relatives have rejected him, so he has no social standing. And don't forget the scandal surrounding his parents' death. Would you want something like that trailing your daughter?"

The other woman was silent.

"No, I did not think so," Ratna continued. "The father was an alcoholic. The boy has probably inherited it. Would you want a drunkard and wife-beater for a future son-in-law?"

Again the other woman was silent.

Amrith stumbled away to his bed and sat down shakily. A feverish heat took hold of him. He had not realized that the circumstances of his parents' death and his father's drunkenness were known in their social circle.

Later, once the women had left, Aunty Bundle came to his room. She wandered around aimlessly, tidying up things on his bookshelf and chest of drawers, before she finally spoke. "Son, you should feel sorry for that woman. The reason she has come back is because her husband has abandoned her for an Australian woman." She shook her head. "I never liked that Ratna, even as a girl. I hope she doesn't visit again or try to thrust her daughters at us."

Aunty Bundle did not look at him while she spoke. She had been confronted, for the first time, by the problem of Amrith's past and the consequences it might have for his future.

After that, Amrith became conscious that people did look at him oddly, when they thought he was unaware of their gaze. And he also began to notice that mothers tended to be watchful when he was talking to their daughters, at the club or after church. He knew that part of this watchfulness was because he was growing into manhood, and so boundaries needed to be put between the sexes. But he also felt sure that another part of their vigilance had to do with his flawed past. Amrith had no interest in girls, and he had never really thought of marriage before. Yet, it frightened him that his past might prove a barrier, when he did want to get married.

Without realizing it, Amrith had got off his bed and gone to his chest of drawers. Opening the top drawer, he took out a leather-bound photo album. A few years after he came to stay with the Manuel-Pillais, Aunty Bundle had given it to him. It contained all the photographs she had of his mother, in the time they had known each other as girls.

The first page was titled *Asha at 12. Holiday in Galle Fort,* and had photographs of his mother about to bat in a cricket field with ramparts in the distance, his mother leaning on a balustrade with her hand against her cheek, his mother and Aunty Bundle on bicycles in a narrow street with houses on either side that had pillared porches. Another page was titled *Asha at 15. Jaffna Holiday,* and showed his mother and Aunty Bundle in identical sun-dresses with spaghetti straps and rows of embroidery and piping on their skirts. They stood with their arms around each other, against a stark sandy background with palmyra trees in the distance. On the same page, they were both in bathing suits having a well bath, flinging pails of water at each other. Another page, *Asha at 10. Ballet,* showed his mother in a ballet costume, striking various poses; in yet another – *Asha in Great Expectations* – his mother was dressed as a man with top hat and tails, the other girls in crinolines. The last picture in the album took up the whole page and it had probably been taken not long before his mother eloped with his father, for she looked like the woman he remembered. It was a studio portrait from the chest upwards. She looked vulnerable and beautiful, her chin lifted exposing her bare neck, her head turned slightly to the left, her frizzy hair pushed back behind an ear that had a pearl on it. She was wearing a checked sari and a blouse with short sleeves.

He shut the album, an angry sound escaping from him. He was sick of the past, just sick of it. He drifted to the French windows and stared out into the side garden. The monsoon shower had abruptly ceased, and there was a silence all around him, broken only by the *drip-drip-drip-ping* of water from the trees and gutters. In the quiet, he could hear the girls in their bedroom, across the side garden. Amrith put on his rubber slippers. He did not want to be alone with his thoughts anymore.

≈≈≈

The girls had seen him coming across the garden, for the moment he stepped in through their French windows, Selvi sprang out from behind the curtains and grabbed him from the rear in a headlock. "What is the password?" she cried, with the glee of an older sister dominating her younger sibling. "You cannot enter without giving the password."

He tried to struggle out of her grip, but Selvi, who remained a tomboy even though she was almost sixteen, held on with great expertise.

Mala, as usual, leapt to Amrith's defence. "Sin, men," she cried at her sister, "leave Amrith alone." She jumped off her bed and tried to rescue him from Selvi's grip, which only mortified Amrith even further.

When they were children, he and Selvi would scuffle frequently, rolling on the floor as they tried to get the best of each other, Amrith often losing. Mala hated their fighting and she would stand by, wringing her hands and weeping, begging her sister to stop hurting him.

"Akka!" Mala tried to come between them. "Leave him alone!"

A significant look passed between the sisters. Selvi immediately released her grip on him. "Sorry, Amrith." She patted his arm. "I forgot that it was —"

A frown from Mala silenced her.

"Forgot what?" Amrith cried, with sudden recklessness. "What did you forget?"

"Nothing," Selvi mumbled, and went to sit at the foot of Mala's bed.

Amrith was furious at them for this delicacy around his mother's death anniversary. He wanted to yell, "Stop pretending this is just another day!" But he could not bring himself to do so.

The girls went back to painting each other's toenails, which they had been doing before his arrival. Selvi looked a little shamefaced as the sisters sat at either end of Mala's bed, their feet in each other's laps.

Looking at them, Amrith felt ragged with envy. It was so unfair that their lives were normal, that nothing stood in the way of their futures. They were free, unshackled by the taint of an awful past. And just by thinking this, a gulf opened up between him and the girls. A gulf that had begun to grow in the last year.

Amrith threw himself down on Selvi's bed. He lay on his side, his head propped by his elbow. "So-so, Selvi, have you heard of Mala's latest ambition?"

Mala flushed with dismay. "Amrith!" she cried, "You promised not to tell. It was a secret."

He could see the hurt flooding her eyes, but he could not stop himself. He wanted to hurt her, as if her pain would bring him relief from his own darkness.

A hideous grin spread across his face. "Guess what our Mala told me?" he said to Selvi.

"What-what?" she asked eagerly.

He paused dramatically. "Our Mala wants to be a nun."

He waited for his words to have their effect. Selvi's eyes widened in astonishment, then she fell back on the bed, clutching her sides and hooting with laughter.

"Amrith," Mala said, close to tears, "I'll never-ever tell you anything again."

Amrith tossed his head in contempt. She always confessed her secrets to him and, even though sooner or later he would betray her in this way, it never stopped her from telling him again.

He told Selvi that Sister Dominica, with whom Mala taught English to poor children in their parish, had recently informed Mala that she might have the gift of a vocation bestowed on her by God. Mala, who was always taking up one scheme or another with great fervor, had been thrilled at this new possibility. She now believed that she was destined to be a nun and had told Amrith that she intended to take her vows the moment she finished her A levels.

All this made Selvi laugh even harder. *"Chee,"* she cried at her sister, "why would you want to do something so ghastly as become a nun? Only dried-up spinsters who can't get married enter the nunnery."

"There are lots of nuns who *choose* to dedicate their life to God, akka," Mala said, with an attempt at dignity.

"What nonsense – life of unhappiness." Selvi tossed her head in disdain.

"I think we should tell Uncle Lucky about Mala's ambition," Amrith said. "He'll be so upset, he's bound to have a talk with that Sister Dominica."

"Amrith! Are you mad? Do you want me to die of mortification?" Mala cried.

"Yes-yes," Selvi said, in her older-sister voice, "Sister Dominica needs a good telling off for leading fourteen-year-old girls like you into a path of such misery. If Amrith doesn't tell Appa, I'm definitely going to inform him."

Mala looked from one to the other with such desperation that they burst out laughing again.

"If you become a nun," Amrith said, "you'll have to cut your hair short and get up at five every morning for the rest of your life."

"And sleep on a hard bed in a dormitory full of other nuns. Not to mention lining up for the toilet, which will probably be a squatting pan." Selvi gestured to the Shaun Cassidy album that lay on Mala's bed. "No pop music. Only dreary hymns."

"And you can forget about seeing films, or going out to Flower Drum for dinner." Amrith, like Selvi, honed in on all the things Mala loved. "No chili crab, anymore."

Mala tried to look superior, but she was beginning to wilt under the reality of what being a nun would mean.

"But most of all," Selvi said, grinning at Amrith, "you can never-ever have a boyfriend."

"Yes-yes," Amrith chimed in, "no Suraj Wanigasekera for you."

"*Chee,* but what are you both talking about?" Mala cried in horror. "Suraj is going to be a priest. He told me so."

They shrieked with laughter. Suraj Wanigasekera was one of the unruliest boys in Amrith's school, always in detention and seated outside the principal's office.

"Yes," Mala cried. "At the last Catholic Students' Union meeting, Suraj told me this."

"Oh, Mala," Selvi said, shaking her head, "you're so gullible. Suraj just said that so you would like him."

"He did not, he did not."

They cackled with derision at the thought of Suraj Wanigasekera as a priest.

And yet Amrith, even as he laughed, was beginning to feel bad about what he had done. Though Mala's ambition was silly, at the same time she had shared a precious dream with him, a dream she was still too shy to share with anyone else. He should have respected her secrecy.

With Selvi, he knew just how far he could go. Being two years older, she looked down on him with the superiority of the senior sister, the akka, and she tried to boss him around. When he resisted, tempers would flare, but a good quarrel would clear the air. Mala, on the other hand, regarded him as an older brother, even though they were the same age. She worshipped him, and he knew that he had the power to wound her in a way he could never do with Selvi. He frequently took advantage of this power.

Before tea, Amrith gruffly invited Mala up to the terrace to help him feed the birds. She went eagerly, ready as always to forgive him.

That evening, there was a meeting of the Catholic Students' Union in the courtyard. Boys from Amrith's school and girls from Mala's.

As Amrith passed by them on the way to his room, they were making plans for a shramadana at an old folks' home, which would involve cleaning, gardening, painting, and entertaining the residents. Suraj Wanigasekera was present, of course. He was a few years older than Amrith, stocky and powerfully built. He was popular with the boys for his debonair, don't-care attitude. As captain of the rugger team, he had scored the winning goal that had garnered for the school the prestigious Sir Hugh Clifford shield.

As Amrith went by the group, Suraj made a suggestion for the shramadana and Mala replied with a little superior laugh, "Oh, Suraj, that is such a silly idea." She gave him a coy look and he grinned with happiness.

It puzzled Amrith that Mala, who was flat-chested and dark-skinned, had such a popular senior boy interested in her, while Selvi, who was fair-skinned, pretty, and well shaped, had no one. Suraj was not the only admirer. Other boys, particularly bad boys, were drawn to Mala. They jostled for her attention at parties and the right to dance

with her; they tried to hold her down in conversation after
church and during school society events. These other
suitors had withdrawn, now that Suraj had staked his claim.

The flirtation between Mala and Suraj would go no
further. Aunty Bundle and Uncle Lucky did not want
Amrith or the girls dating until they were eighteen. Their
teenage years were a time to experience many things
without being tied to the obligation, the narrowness, of a
relationship. Amrith and the girls obeyed this rule. It was
a great privilege that their parents sanctioned dating at any
age. Their friends and classmates envied them this future
liberty. Most of them would have arranged marriages.
Others might be allowed to date in their twenties, if the
partner was first vetted to be of the right caste, class, religion, and race, with good education and prospects.

For some unknown reason, the courtyard was always relatively free of mosquitoes, which were plentiful at this time
of year. If it was not raining, the family always sat out here
before dinner. Uncle Lucky's driver, Soma, and Amrith
would carry two Planter's chairs to one end of the courtyard
for Aunty Bundle and Uncle Lucky. Then they would place
a rattan table and three chairs for Amrith and the girls at the
other end. While the adults had their drinks and caught up
on their day, Amrith and the girls would play a board game –
Chinese Checkers, or Carom, or Scrabble.

Today, however, Amrith helped Soma arrange all the
chairs together in a circle. The family was going to meet
and discuss the upcoming birthday party. Both Selvi and

Mala were born in early September, two years and five days apart. They always had a joint party. This year, Selvi was turning sixteen and it was to be an especially grand event, the most looked-forward-to social occasion of the holidays among their friends. The monsoon storm last night, however, had created an obstacle to the upcoming celebrations, causing much anxiety to Selvi and Mala. If the roof was not mended in time, there would be no party.

Once Jane-Nona had lit mosquito coils under the chairs and brought out a metal candelabra, the family took their seats and started to discuss the upcoming party. They had barely begun when they heard a car at their gate and Aunt Wilhelmina calling out in her fluting voice, "Hilloo, hilloo."

Amrith ran to open the gate.

The old lady was Aunty Bundle's aunt. She often dropped by the Manuel-Pillais' for meals. Despite her enormous wealth, she was a lonely woman, being childless and a widow.

When Amrith came out onto the road, Aunt Wilhelmina was still seated in her car, waiting for the driver to come around and open her door. Once he had done so, she stepped out. She had come from an embassy party and was impeccably turned out in a maroon silk dress, her handbag, belt, and shoes in the same material. A finely wrought ruby necklace graced her neck and she had on matching ruby earrings, broach, and bracelet. Her dark blonde hair was done up in a French pleat at the back and her fair European complexion, of which she was so exceedingly proud, was lightly touched up with foundation to make it even whiter.

When she saw Amrith, she beamed. He was her particular favorite. "Child, when are you coming to visit me? All
my silver and ornaments are in dire need of a good cleaning. And I refuse to trust anybody with them, but you.
Now that you have your holidays, you must come."

"Yes, Aunt Wilhelmina, I will."

She patted him on the shoulder and sailed into the
courtyard.

"*Ah,*" she said, as she came up to the family, "this
monsoon certainly turns us upside down." She kissed her
niece on her cheeks. "How did you survive yesterday's
storm? All my bougainvilleas are in ruin."

Aunty Bundle told her what had happened to their
roof.

"Gracious," Aunt Wilhelmina said, taking a seat among
them, "how awful." She glanced at the girls. "And with your
party coming up, too. I do hope the hole can be mended in
time. Roofers are as rare as hen's teeth these days. My dear
friend, Lady Rajapakse, has been waiting for a month."

The girls looked panicked.

"Bundle," Uncle Lucky said, "have you sent for the
roofers?"

"This very afternoon I sent a telegram to Gineris and
his sons," Aunty Bundle replied. "Don't worry, they will
come. Gineris has been working for my family since I was
a girl. He will not let me down."

"Perhaps I should make inquiries about other roofers,
just in case," Uncle Lucky said.

"No-no." Aunty Bundle's face set in a stubborn line. "I'm not letting any old roof-baas fix the hole."

They all looked at her doubtfully and Aunt Wilhelmina said, "I would search for other roof-baases. You never know." She looked around at the children. "And what are you doing for your holidays, my dears?"

Mala told the old lady that she would be spending every morning in the parish hall helping Sister Dominica teach English to slum children. While she did so, she glanced anxiously at Selvi and Amrith, who smirked back at her, but did not bring up her ambition to be a nun.

Selvi, it seemed, had all sorts of plans for her holiday – various spend-the-days at friends' houses, day trips to a hotel that was owned by a friend's father, a carnival they wanted to attend. She was a popular girl in school, junior netball star, on the track to house captain and head girl. She was part of a close-knit circle of friends who were also well-liked sporty girls. Suhashini, Nayantara, Otara, and Tanuja – from whose names, Amrith had coined the delicious acronym SNOT. The other students clamored for the attention of Selvi and the SNOTs, and they had received a host of invitations and had been able to choose among them. All her plans, however, would have to be fitted around the private tuition classes she had to attend every morning. Her midyear marks had been terrible, not to mention all the pranks she had pulled.

Aunty Bundle had been summoned twice to the school office by the Mother Superior. The first instance was when Selvi, on a dare, rode a cow that had been brought in to crop the grass on the school playground. The second was when Selvi, following a seminar on menstruation by a Kotex representative, had worn the sample sanitary pad around her neck in lieu of a school tie.

"And Amrith," Aunt Wilhelmina said, turning to him. "What are your plans, dear?"

"Um . . . nothing much, Aunty."

"Well, there is your typing," Uncle Lucky reminded him.

"And don't forget your school play," Mala added.

# 5

# Othello

~~~~~~~~

Every year, schools in Colombo, and a few in Kandy, competed in the much-anticipated Inter-School Shakespeare Competition, in which each school performed a scene from a Shakespearean play. Since none of the schools were coed, the female roles were usually played by juniors in the boys' schools, and the male roles played by seniors in the girls' schools. There were separate prizes for each gender. Last year, Amrith had played Juliet and won the cup for Best Female Portrayal from a Boys' School. Aunty Bundle and the girls had been ecstatic over his success, but no one was prouder than Uncle Lucky at seeing Amrith win the cup for his alma mater.

Usually, rehearsals for the Shakespeare Competition began after the August holidays, with the event being held in the last week of November. This year, however, the competition was to be held earlier. The British Council was bringing over a one-man show by an actor from the Royal Shakespeare Company in England. This actor had graciously agreed to judge the competition. To suit his schedule, the event was going to be held in early October.

There was much excitement over the prospect of having a real professional actor from such a prestigious company as the judge. An added aura of glamor hung over the competition, and each school was even more determined to win all the cups. The drama teacher and students at Amrith's school had all agreed that they should meet a few times over the August holidays to rehearse; that this sacrifice must be made to try and win honor for the school colors.

Rehearsing in the holidays was no sacrifice at all for Amrith. He was greatly looking forward to it, as a relief from the tedium of the empty days ahead. He was also very excited at the prospect of a real Shakespearean actor judging the competition. After he had won the cup last year, he had begun to secretly entertain the idea of becoming an actor. He often fantasized about being in various shows and the numerous curtain calls he would receive.

He had already got a taste for this applause and what it meant to have a reputation as a successful actor. Before he won the cup last year, he had been the kind of boy that other students ignored. Nobody spoke to him and he was never included in any after-school activities, nor invited to birthday parties. Like all invisible boys, Amrith had kept as indistinguishable as possible. He knew that if he did get attention, it would only be negative. All that had changed with his winning the cup. First, there had been the moment when the cup was presented to him by the principal, at an assembly in front of the whole school. As he went up on the stage, the entire student body had roared its approval at his winning this glory for their school, boys in his class whistling and calling, "Well done, Amrith, well done." He had been surprised and touched by this tribute. After that, though his classmates still did not include him in their various activities, they always greeted him with respect and often asked his opinion on matters of art and literature. Most of the other boys in the play had been seniors, a few of them prefects. Amrith had worried that his shyness and silence would be made fun of, but these older boys actually liked him for his quietness and saw it as a sign of deference to their higher status. When these senior boys met him in the corridors, they always greeted him warmly, whereas they ignored the other junior boys.

This year, Amrith's school was doing the last scene from *Othello*. There had been a meeting of the Drama Society, just before school ended, and the boys had talked about which parts they were going to try out for. From this discussion, Amrith understood that there were three roles that would go automatically to the students who wanted them, since no one else would be auditioning for those parts. Thus Othello belonged to Mala's admirer, Suraj Wanigasekera; Emilia to a boy named Fernando; and Desdemona, Othello's wife, to Amrith.

He was thrilled at the prospect of playing such a major role and he was determined to win the cup again. The thought of being declared the best by an English

Shakespearean actor would be further confirmation that he was destined to be an actor.

Amrith could not be bothered to struggle through the Elizabethan English of the play to find out the plot. Instead, he went into the library in their home and took down a book that had Shakespearean plays retold in modern prose. He returned to his room with the book and lay on his bed, reading the story of Othello.

It was a tale, so the subtitle to the story declared, "of jealousy and its tragic consequences." Othello, the main character, was a Moor, a black man. He was a successful warrior and had been promoted to High General of the Venetian forces by the Duke of Venice. His greatest enemy was his ensign, Iago, who was jealous of Othello's success, but also angry and envious that Othello had chosen one Michael Cassio to be his second-in-command over Iago. Iago set out to destroy Othello. While pretending to be Othello's closest friend, he preyed on a great weakness the Moor had – his love for his wife, Desdemona. Othello's love was so powerful that it made him vulnerable. Because he could not imagine a life without Desdemona, the threat of her deceiving him, or leaving him, lay in wait to trap him. Iago began to exploit this weakness. He used Michael Cassio – who was extremely good-looking – to do so. Othello had given Desdemona a handkerchief when they were courting. She had accidentally dropped it and her lady-in-waiting, Emilia, who was also Iago's wife, had found it. Iago forced Emilia to give it to him. He planted it in

Cassio's room, then told Othello that he had seen the fateful handkerchief in Cassio's hand. Iago also told Othello that he had shared a bed with Cassio one night, and Cassio had murmured in his sleep of his love for Desdemona and cursed the Moor for having her. Othello demanded the handkerchief from Desdemona, but she could not produce it. He began to believe that his wife was being unfaithful to him with Cassio. Iago, through other tricks, inflamed the Moor's jealousy until he was finally convinced that his wife had betrayed him.

Thus began the final scene in *Othello,* the one that Amrith's school was doing. It took place in Desdemona's bedroom. In the middle of the night, Othello, mad with jealousy, entered and woke his wife. He accused a bewildered Desdemona of infidelity with Cassio. She vehemently denied it and tried to reason with him. Yet, her husband was blind to all reasoning and he told her to say her prayers before he killed her. She begged for her life, but Othello would grant her no mercy. He smothered her to death with a pillow.

A large part of the scene was taken up with their exchange. The only other role of any great weight was that of Emilia, who, on hearing noises from her mistress' room, came in to investigate. When she saw Desdemona killed, she screamed for help. Lodovico, a Venetian nobleman, along with his attendants and other courtiers, came to her assistance. Iago was with them. When Othello told them his reasons for killing Desdemona, mentioning the handkerchief, Emilia saw what her husband had done. She told Othello the truth. Iago, in order to silence his wife, stabbed her in the side, killing her. He fled the room, but was brought back by guards. Cassio now entered and Othello understood the terrible mistake he had made. Out of remorse, but also to preserve his dignity as a great warrior, he took his life as the play ended.

Once Amrith had finished reading the story of Othello, he carefully went through the last scene of the play, using a dictionary to help with the difficult Elizabethan English. He was delighted by Desdemona's role. There was lots of room for great acting in this part. He decided that, since the role of Desdemona was already his, he would memorize it, thus getting an early start on his chance of winning the cup. When he felt he had mastered his lines, he went looking for Mala to run through them with her.

She was in her favorite reading spot, on the caned divan in the living room, her legs drawn up to her chest, the book propped on her knees. There was a bowl of nellis by her and, not taking her eye off the page, she was dipping each fruit in a mixture of salt and chili powder before popping it in her mouth, her lips puckering at its tartness. She was deeply absorbed in George Elliot's *Mill on the Floss,* but she put it away, flushing with pleasure and importance as Amrith held out his copy of *Othello* to her. While she was better at reading the other parts than Selvi, the real reason Amrith asked her was that he enjoyed the admiring way she looked at him as he declaimed his lines, the note of worship in her eyes.

That evening, the drama teacher called to remind Amrith that there were to be auditions and a preliminary rehearsal the following day. After Amrith put down the telephone, he was lost in thought.

It was a custom in his school to address every female teacher as Madam, and yet when boys, particularly former students, spoke of Madam, they only meant one teacher – Mrs. Algama, who taught English Literature and Greek and Roman Civilization at the A level and who also ran the Drama Society, or Dramsoc as it was commonly known. Mrs. Algama, or Madam, was a plump, short woman with a brisk manner who wore a Kandyan sari, the palu wrapped around her waist in a no-nonsense style. She was adored by her students and held in higher regard than any other teacher in their school. This was because, in a curious way, she was one of the boys. She would joke with them and sometimes tease a boy in a good-natured manner, particularly someone who had given himself airs and graces, for which she had no patience. She was the only teacher the boys dared tell suggestive jokes to and while she pretended to be shocked – waving her handkerchief at them in horror, pressing the edge of her palu to her mouth – they were not fooled. Her husband was a well-known Sinhalese stage actor. They moved in the artistic, bohemian circles of Colombo. There was very little that actually shocked Madam.

Amrith felt curiously uneasy around Madam. She had a way of looking at him, as if she saw right into his soul and understood something about him that he did not understand about himself. And what she saw made her more kind to him, more gentle. She never joked or teased him, or used her wit against him. And yet her gentleness made him all the more uncomfortable.

~~~~~

The next morning, instead of going to the office to practice typing, Amrith had Uncle Lucky drop him off at his school. He stood for a moment before the gates, looking at the main building at the end of the driveway. It had rained hard in the early hours and there were great puddles in the driveway, steaming in the heat of the sun. The building squatted beyond this haze, its whitewash a sickened yellow in the sunlight. The massive stone arch at the entrance looked like an enormous mouth, the corpulent domes at either end like unblinking eyes. Usually the sight of the building made Amrith feel gloomy, but today he was filled with excitement at the day of rehearsals ahead; filled with anticipation of the success that could be his in a few months. He pushed open the gates and went up the driveway.

When he came into the building, the ghostly silence made him hasten through the foyer, the photographs of former principals glowering down on him. As he made his way down a cavernous corridor, his footsteps echoed and once or twice he turned, almost sure someone was walking behind him. He was approaching the auditorium and he could hear voices. As he drew nearer, there was a burst of laughter from within, followed by hooting and catcalls.

He entered to find the other boys seated halfway down the auditorium, involved in a conversation that was causing them much merriment. "*Ah,* De Alwis," they called out, addressing him by his surname, as was the custom in the school.

He went down the central aisle towards them, his face frozen in a shy smile. Madam had not yet arrived.

Mala's admirer, Suraj Wanigasekera, was amongst the boys and he called to Amrith in a commanding tone, "Now come and sit with us, De Alwis."

The last time Amrith had seen Suraj, he had been on his best behavior, at his most humble. Now his demeanor was more in tune with his real character. He was lording it over the others, his arms spread out over the two chairs on either side, his feet up on the chair in front of him, the other boys gathered around.

Except for a few boys from the junior forms who were playing the supernumeraries – guards, courtiers, and so forth, who would come in at the end – all the boys were seniors. Besides Suraj, there was a razor-thin debater named Ahmed, who was sure to get the part of Iago. The boy playing Iago's wife, Emilia, was called Fernando. He was a tubby, good-humored boy who was brilliant in English Literature and the Classics and was destined for

Oxford when he finished his A levels. He was Madam's right-hand man and was in charge of the set, costumes, and props. Jayasingha, the assistant head prefect, was seated next to Suraj. They were close friends.

Amrith had almost reached the circle of boys when he noticed, a little away from the others, a boy named Peries, whom he had not seen in quite a while. Amrith stopped in surprise. Peries used to be in the Dramsoc but, after he joined an American evangelical church last year, he had declined to have anything to do with plays, which he considered sinful.

The other boys had no fondness for Peries, whom they often referred to as Penis. It was clear they had been teasing him from the look of sullen petulance on his face, his arms folded to his chest.

As Amrith took his place among them, Suraj said, "Yes-yes, Penis, your soul is going to be damned in hell for wanting to be in our play."

"I say, Penis, don't you know that, in the old days, actors were buried outside the graveyard because they were considered sinners?" Jayasingha winked at Suraj. "You're polluting your soul, just being around us."

"*And,*" Suraj added, "you want to try for a woman's role? Surely, you will burn eternally in hell for that."

The boys laughed uproariously.

Amrith stared at Peries and a cold dismay took hold of him. Peries had always played female roles. In fact, he had been slated to play Juliet last year, but he had left halfway through the rehearsal period because of his new religious scruples. Which female part was Peries going to try for?

Amrith was distracted from his thoughts by Madam's arrival. She bustled in, her handbag under her arm, and hurried down the aisle, moping her brow and temples with a handkerchief. "Sorry I'm late, boys. My trishaw man took forever to come and pick me up. *Ah,* we're all here? Good-good." Then she saw Peries and stopped in astonishment.

"Well," she said, and a small smile appeared on her face, "Peries. What a surprise."

He stood up sheepishly and she crooked her finger at him to come forward. "So, Peries," she said, looking at him, her head to one side, "are you here to try out for the play?"

He nodded without meeting her eyes.

"I see. And may I ask which role?"

He did not answer for a moment. Amrith leaned forward in his seat, holding his breath.

Peries looked up at Madam. "Desdemona."

Amrith sat back. A sigh of dismay escaped from him.

"Well." Madam, who had heard Amrith's sigh, glanced at him. "I haven't assigned the parts yet, so any boy is free to try for whatever role he wants."

She was going to say something further to Peries, but then patted his shoulder. "It's nice to have you back, Peries. Religion, you know, cannot solve all life's problems." There was a look of pity in Madam's eyes. Peries' parents had divorced last year.

Madam signaled to Fernando and they went up onstage. Some of the other boys followed and began to help lay out

the bed and additional furniture that would make up
Desdemona's room. Amrith sat where he was, too numb to
move. He had imagined himself onstage in front of the
audience, giving a wonderful performance; had imagined
that moment when the English actor would name him for
Best Female Portrayal from a Boys' School. He glanced
over at Peries – who was poring over his copy of *Othello* –
and narrowed his eyes at his bent head. It was he, Amrith,
who had saved the school's honor last year. If he had not
stepped into the role and given such a fine performance,
they would have probably lost the most important cup for
Best Play to their arch-rival, St. Stephen's. Now Peries was
planning to return and take up where he had so summarily
left off. Amrith could not help feeling angry at Madam.
She was being too scrupulously fair. Peries had, after all,
left her in the lurch last year. She need not grant him a
chance at the part.

Peries, drawn by Amrith's gaze, looked towards him. He
raised his eyebrows challengingly and sneered, as if to say
that he did not consider Amrith any challenge at all.
Amrith hastily lowered his eyes. He was suddenly nervous.

The scene had been set up. Madam and the boys came
down from the stage and the auditions began.

Amrith sat with the others in the auditorium as boys
went up onstage and tried out for the various roles. As each
minute passed, he could feel his nervousness increase. His
mouth felt dry and a coldness ran up and down his spine.
As he glanced at his rival, he could not help dwelling on the
fact that, in past years, Peries had frequently walked away

with the cup for Best Female Portrayal. He was up against stiff competition. He could end up losing the part.

Finally, there were only two roles left to be cast. Desdemona and Cassio. Madam turned in her seat and regarded Amrith and Peries. "Now, boys, the one who doesn't get Desdemona will be assigned to Cassio."

And then Amrith truly understood what was at stake. Cassio was a minor role in this scene, with just a few lines. If he got Cassio, he would have no chance of winning any prize. He would return to being a nonentity in his school.

Madam asked both Peries and Amrith to go backstage and wait to be called. Even though he had learnt the lines thoroughly, Amrith took his copy of *Othello* with him. Peries, however, left his copy behind. He, too, had memorized the part. He strode down the aisle towards the stage, his head held high, a smirk on his face that said the role was already his. Amrith followed. His hands were slick with sweat and he rubbed them against the sides of his trousers.

When they were backstage, Peries, who was one year older, looked Amrith up and down with contempt and said, "You shouldn't waste your time, De Alwis. I have played many more roles than you in the Dramsoc. You might have won for Juliet last year, but I won in both the previous years for Portia and Ophelia."

Amrith, already aware of this, felt even more nervous. He licked his lips. "I . . . I . . . ."

"You, you, what?" sneered Peries. "Can't even speak properly and you want to be an actor?" He tossed his head in disdain.

Before Amrith could respond, Madam called him onto the stage. She instructed him to lie down on the bed and pretend to be asleep. Once he was in place, she signaled for Suraj to start his monologue. Amrith, as he lay there, became aware that his hands were shaking. He pressed them against his sides to try and steady them.

Suraj came to the end of his monologue. He bent over the bed and pretended to kiss Amrith. It was Amrith's cue to awaken. He stirred, opened his eyes, and looked up at Suraj. He was waiting for Amrith to say his first line. Amrith stared at him. In the silence, he could hear a crow cawing in the school garden. His mind was blank.

"Your text, De Alwis," Suraj said softly, with an inclination of his head to the copy of *Othello* lying by the bed.

Amrith quickly picked up his book and glanced at the first line. *"Who's there? Othello?"* His voice was barely audible. That moment of blankness had rattled him and he could not seem to find his equilibrium.

*"Ay, Desdemona,"* Suraj replied.

Amrith cleared his throat loudly. *"Will you . . . come to bed, my lord?"*

*"Have you prayed tonight, Desdemona?"*

*"Ay, my lord."* Amrith could tell he was doing terribly, his voice colorless and weak.

*"If you bethink yourself of any crime*
*Unreconciled as yet to heaven and grace,*
*Solicit for it straight,"* Suraj said.

*"Alack, my lord, what may you mean by that?"* Amrith realized that his arms were shaking again, the book

jiggling in his hand. He pressed his elbow against his side
to steady himself.

Suraj continued on with his lines.

*"Well, do it and be brief. I will walk by,*
*I would not kill thy unprepared spirit.*
*No, heaven forfend, I will not —"*

There was a crash as Amrith's book slipped between his
fingers and fell to the floor. He leapt out of bed and hurriedly searched around for it in the semidarkness of the
stage. He finally found his *Othello* and straightened up.

"Do you want to start again, De Alwis?" Madam called
out from the front row.

He nodded dumbly. He went to take his position again
on the bed. As he passed Suraj, the senior patted him on the
shoulder and whispered, "We're all rooting for you, De
Alwis. Just relax and you'll be fine."

But Amrith was too upset by now to salvage his performance. He went through the audition, his voice pale and
lifeless, his acting wooden.

Finally it was over.

"Thank you, De Alwis." There was a kindness in
Madam's voice that deadened him.

Amrith stumbled towards the steps that led down into
the auditorium. Peries was crossing the stage at the same
time and, as he passed Amrith, he smiled triumphantly.

Peries strutted over to the bed, lay down, and signaled
Suraj that he could start his monologue whenever he wanted.

The moment Peries said his first line, Amrith knew he
had lost the part.

When Peries was finally done, there was silence in the auditorium. The silence of resignation. All the boys saw that the role would have to go to Peries.

The auditions were now over. Madam, along with her right-hand man, Fernando, went out of the auditorium to discuss the casting of roles. Amrith stared at the floor, knowing that he had lost Desdemona and would be assigned Cassio.

After a short while, Madam and Fernando returned. She called to the boys and they gathered around her. She began to read out the cast, leaving the roles of Desdemona and Cassio until the end. After she had assigned all the other parts, Madam was silent, looking at her hands. "With regards to Desdemona, I feel the need to make some explanation about my choice." She glanced around at them. "De Alwis, as you all saw, did not do well, although he is a good actor. Peries, on the other hand, gave an excellent audition. It is fair that he be given the role."

Amrith clutched his hands together tightly, his fingernails digging into his palms. There was a murmur of disappointment from the other boys.

Madam held up her hand to indicate she was not finished. "On the other hand, I am sure you remember how Peries left us in the lurch, a few weeks before our performance of *Romeo and Juliet*. If it wasn't for De Alwis stepping into the role and doing a magnificent job, our school would have lost to St. Stephen's."

The boys nodded in agreement.

"As you know," Madam continued, "this is a very important year, with a judge from the Royal Shakespeare Company no less. I cannot afford to take the chance that anything might go wrong. Peries' audition was superior, but can we rely on him?"

They all watched her expectantly. Amrith leaned forward in his seat.

"The role of Desdemona thus goes to De Alwis –"

The boys cheered and Amrith gasped, hardly able to believe what he had heard. They began to pat him on the back, and he blushed with joy and pleasure.

Madam called for them to be silent. "Boys, I am not done yet. I wanted to say that the role of Desdemona goes to De Alwis only for now."

Amrith frowned, not understanding.

"Peries will be assigned Cassio, but will also learn the role of Desdemona and shadow De Alwis. Then, in a few weeks, based on how you do, De Alwis, the role will remain yours or not."

Amrith felt his euphoria diminish. He would have to prove himself or he could end up with Cassio. He silently vowed that he would work very hard and not lose the role of Desdemona.

The boys were going out to a restaurant for lunch. Before they left, Amrith went to use the toilet and, when he came back, he found that they were teasing Peries again – this time about the role of Cassio. Amrith, having missed a part of the conversation, was not sure what exactly the ragging was about, but Peries was clearly disturbed, though he was trying his best to hide it.

"But you know, Penis, I'm not making it up," Jayasingha, the assistant head prefect said, with a conspiratorial look at Suraj, who winked back. "The lines about Cassio lying with Iago in bed are right there in act 3, scene 3. Turn to it and see for yourself. It's in bold print."

"I don't believe you." Peries shook his head.

"*Aday*, Penis, didn't you read the whole play before you came for rehearsal?" Ahmed, who was to play Iago, asked. "Everybody else read the whole play."

The boys nodded, though Amrith doubted they had. Seeing the smug look on Fernando's face, Amrith suspected that he was the only one who had read the play. Fernando had, no doubt, alerted the other boys to whatever went on in act 3, scene 3.

Suraj gestured at Peries. "I say, open your damn book and see for yourself, men."

Peries did not do so. He stood up, said he was going to the toilet, and left. The other boys watched him go, then grinned at each other. They gave him a few moments. Then Suraj and Jayasingha crept out. There was a shout of triumph, a hoot of laughter. They came back followed by a shamefaced Peries, Suraj holding up Peries' copy of *Othello* that he had been flipping through in the corridor. The other boys laughed and began to whistle, making kissing sounds at Peries. Ahmed tried to embrace Peries. "Cassio, you can lie with me anytime."

Peries pushed him away and stormed out of the auditorium, followed by catcalls and hoots. Amrith had no
idea what they were teasing Peries about, but he could not
help feeling glad to see his rival discomfited.

Amrith discovered that Madam, too, understood the joke
about Cassio.

When they had returned to the auditorium after lunch,
and were seated in a circle, ready to do a read-through, Peries
raised his hand and said, "Madam, I wish to give up my part."

All the boys tittered and a mischievous glint entered
Madam's eyes. "And why is that, Peries? Cassio is a very
good role."

The boys giggled. Some of them guffawed.

"Peries," Madam continued, "you are perfect for Cassio.
I need someone who is poetic looking. And you have such
lovely fair skin, such pretty curls."

The boys clutched their sides with silent hilarity; some
of them had tears running down their faces. Even Amrith
could not help smiling, though he still did not know what
this was all about.

Peries' face was red from having to bite back his fury.
"But I don't want to do it, Madam. I would rather play a
guard than play Cassio."

"Nonsense," Madam said, opening her copy of *Othello*.
"I don't want to hear any more about this, Peries.
Wanigasekera, read!"

Since there was still a possibility Amrith could end up playing Cassio, he had a look at act 3, scene 3, the moment he got home. It was the point in the plot when Iago told Othello that he had shared a bed with Cassio, and how, during the night, Cassio had murmured in his sleep of his love for Desdemona and cursed Othello for having her. Iago also told Othello that Cassio mistook Iago for Desdemona and held Iago's hand in his, kissed him hard on the lips over and over again, embraced him, and pressed his leg over Iago's thigh.

Amrith was sure this was what the boys had teased Peries about. He did not understand why Peries was so outraged by what Cassio had done mistakenly in his sleep. Still, Amrith felt even more uneasy now about ending up with that part.

Madam was going away with her family for a holiday and there would be no further rehearsals for three weeks. Amrith promised himself that he would use this time to work diligently on his role.

# 6

# The Holidays Drag On

~~~~~~

The climate in August depended on whether the monsoon had spent itself or not; whether it had arrived at all. This year, the monsoon was late and it lingered into August, much to everyone's despair. Instead of the rain cooling down the heat, it only caused the air to be thick with moisture. The inhabitants of Colombo moved sluggishly, as if pushing at the yellow humidity before them. The lush growth in the gardens and on the sides of the streets was rotting with too much water, the hibiscus a diluted pink.

Over the next few days, Amrith found that, without rehearsals, time hung heavy on him. In the past, he and the girls would do things together during their holidays, like going for bicycle rides and walks along the beach, or to a film at the Majestic Cinema and to Gillo's for ice-cream sundaes. But in the last year, as the girls grew older, they had begun to develop their own interests and social circles

into which he did not fit. Amrith felt he had been abandoned
by the girls; he could not help being angry at them and
secretly envious of their busy lives. He rehearsed his part as
much as he could, but he soon grew bored with repeating the
lines over and over to himself. Somehow the scene did not
really work, addressing an imaginary Othello.

His mornings at the office, practicing his typing, were
the sole source of pleasure and distraction in his life.
Though he had been acquainted with the office staff before,
it was only now that he began to know about their lives –
their husbands and wives, their children, their hobbies and
interests. Uncle Lucky's relationship with Miss Rani
remained a mystery, and he often pondered over it. He
would watch them together, remarking to himself on their
intimacy, which appeared almost unseemly between a boss
and his staff member. When they were in a meeting, Uncle
Lucky, as opposed to sitting on his side of the desk with
Miss Rani across from him, would often come around and
sit by her. They would discuss a business problem or a new
venture with their heads bent close together. Uncle Lucky
would sometimes touch Miss Rani's arm in a gesture of
approval and yet, Amrith did not think there was anything
lascivious about this contact. Uncle Lucky often left his
cubicle door open and the rest of the staff could see them.
They appeared unfazed by this intimacy.

To relieve his boredom, Amrith went to visit Aunt
Wilhelmina one afternoon. He found her playing bridge on
the front veranda with her usual coterie of Cinnamon

Gardens dowagers – Lady Rajapakse, Mrs. Zarina Akbarally, and Mrs. Jayalukshmi Coomaraswamy. Amrith was a bit frightened of these formidable women, who never hesitated to speak their minds in a very blunt manner. Yet they were always nice to him and often commented on what a polite boy he was, wishing that their grandsons were more like him.

Once he had greeted them, Aunt Wilhelmina, who was very pleased to see him, led Amrith through the drawing room and dining room, waiting for him to make his choice from her glass-fronted cabinets. He picked the one containing the silver. Aunt Wilhelmina unlocked the doors, then rang a bell for her retainer, Ramu. He laid out newspapers on the dining table and brought in the silver polish and some rags. Amrith was left to his work with a glass of sweetened lime juice, bridge sandwiches, and little iced cakes.

He did not understand why, but bringing back the luster to silver or dusting carefully around the ridges and indentations of porcelain ornaments brought him great contentment. As he took each silver object from the cabinet to the table, he marveled at its beauty – the two elaborate candelabrums, their bases and knops molded with leaves, their serpentine branches ornamented with foliage; a set of dinner plates with a design of acanthus shells and anthemion ornaments etched along the edge; the cake-basket with its finely pierced sides engraved with foliage, flowers, beading, and trelliswork; a bulbous soup tureen with elaborately cast rose finials and rose bracket handles; a tea and coffee service from China carved with panels of Chinese landscapes, the spouts on the pots fashioned to resemble bamboo.

Amrith worked for a while, then needing a break, he walked around the drawing room admiring the furniture. Aunt Wilhelmina had been married in the early 1920s and all her furniture was Art Deco imported from France.

She had a nicely illustrated book on Art Deco furniture and Amrith, as he often did, took it down from the bookshelf and looked through the pages, glancing up every so often at the pieces of furniture to see, in three-dimension, the simple forms and classical styles, the exotic materials and fine handcraftsmanship, the complicated inlays of ivory, tortoiseshell, gold leaf, and tooled leather, the contrasting veneers of rare and expensive wood, which was Art Deco.

~~~~

With nothing much to do, Amrith spent hours in the aviary. While some of this time was devoted to cleaning up and rearranging the perches, what he mostly did was try and train Kuveni to speak. He borrowed a few books from the British Council Library on breeding birds and read up on how to make a bird talk. Yet, despite using all the techniques in the books, he had no success. Kuveni remained stubbornly silent.

The mynah had been a gift to him from Aunty Bundle's friend and partner, the architect Lucien Lindamulagé. Amrith was very fond of the old man and they had spent many mornings of his childhood together in the architect's aviary. It was Lucien Lindamulagé who had found the mynah, when they had been working on a project outstation, and brought it as a gift.

Amrith had been planning to visit Lucien Lindamulagé and consult him on Kuveni's silence when, one evening, he came home from a solitary bicycle ride by the sea to find the old man seated in a Planter's chair in the courtyard, having tea with Aunty Bundle.

Lucien Lindamulagé waved the moment he saw Amrith. "*Ah,* my dear, how marvelously healthy and flushed you look," he cried archly. "No doubt you've been taking in the bracing air of the ocean."

He was a little gray-haired gnome of a man, with large ears and nose, and thick glasses. He always applied white powder to his face, and this gave his dark complexion a grayish sheen. He was seated in a manner not at all befitting his age. His feet were up on the chair, tucked under his white sarong, and his knees were drawn to his chest.

There was something scandalous about Lucien Lindamulagé that Amrith did not understand. It had to do with his constant round of young male secretaries. Amrith had once overheard Uncle Lucky warning his wife that Lucien Lindamulagé should leave his secretaries at home when they went on business outstation; that what the old man did was illegal and he could end up getting arrested. Aunty Bundle had been furious at her husband for believing such rumors. Yet, from the heat of her anger, Amrith felt she knew the rumors were true and was deeply saddened and troubled by whatever it was her friend did.

As Amrith parked his bicycle and went across the courtyard, Lucien Lindamulagé watched his approach over the
edge of his glasses, a merry twinkle in his eyes. When
Amrith was by him, the architect reached up and pulled on
his earlobe affectionately. "Growing taller and taller every
month, *nah*."

Amrith could not help grinning. Despite Lucien
Lindamulagé's odd manner and the scandal surrounding
him, he really liked the old architect. Unlike with most
men, Amrith felt that he could simply be himself around
Lucien Lindamulagé.

"Now tell me," the old man said, squeezing Amrith's
arm, "how are the birds? Has the mynah talked yet?"

Amrith shook his head.

The architect frowned. "How very odd, my dear. What
techniques have you been using?"

Amrith told him all the things he had tried, hoping the
architect would be able to suggest something else, but Lucien
Lindamulagé shook his head. He put his feet on the ground
and stood up. "*Hmm,* let us take a look." He held on to
Amrith's arm, for he did not have his walking stick with him,
and they began to make their way across the courtyard.

Once they were in the aviary, Lucien Lindamulagé tried
to get the mynah to talk, but nothing he did worked either.
He stared at the bird, puzzled for a long time, then his face
lit up. "*Ah!* Perhaps it is loneliness that makes our Kuveni
mute. She needs a mate." He nodded. "Yes-yes. I'm sure
that is the solution."

He turned to Amrith. "We are going outstation in a few days and I will keep my eye out for a male mynah. Village children are adept at catching these birds and will readily give them up for a few rupees."

Amrith looked at Kuveni, who was regarding them as usual with her head to one side, and he hoped that Lucien Lindamulagé's solution might turn out to be correct.

When they came down to the courtyard, Lucien Lindamulagé's secretary was waiting for him – a young man in his midtwenties with an olive skin, glossy black hair, and full lips. As Amrith looked at him, he remembered how he had once heard boys in his school mention Lucien Lindamulagé's secretaries and refer to the old man as a "ponnaya" – a word whose precise meaning Amrith did not understand, though he knew it disparaged the masculinity of another man, reducing him to the level of a woman.

~~~~~
~~~~~

The hole in the living room roof had still not been fixed and, one evening, the family stood around the barrel, which had been placed under the hole to catch the rain, squinting up at the rafters.

"Bundle," Uncle Lucky said, staring up at the hole, "haven't you heard anything yet from Gineris and his sons?"

"Of course I have, Lucky," Aunty Bundle replied, a little defensively. "Mendis and I even drove out to their village. They've promised to come next week."

"But they did not respond to your initial telegram," Uncle Lucky said. "You know how these village-types are, so lackadaisical. Next week can end up being next month. Why don't I try and get another roof-baas. I have a good reference for one who lives right here in Colombo."

Aunty Bundle shook her head, stubbornly.

"*Aiyo,* Amma," Selvi cried at her, "just get this other roof-baas, for goodness' sake."

"No, no," Aunty Bundle said. "Gineris will come. I trust him."

"But what if he doesn't come before the party?" Mala demanded plaintively. "We will have to cancel our birthday. People can't dance with a barrel in the middle of the living room."

"Gineris and his sons have always been our family baases," Aunty Bundle said, folding her arms to her chest. "They will not let me down. Besides, I don't trust these modern baases; they don't know how to lay out tiles in the old style."

"Rubbish, Bundle." Uncle Lucky gave her an exasperated look. "Tiles are tiles. Of course any roof-baas knows how to do it."

Selvi gestured with disgust to the open rafters and handmade red clay tiles of their roof. "I wish we lived in a modern house with proper asbestos roofing and a ceiling."

Aunty Bundle turned to her, annoyed. "You children don't appreciate what you have. This house is a proper Sri Lankan house, not one of those awful Western models that are so unsuitable for the heat." She was on one of her favorite hobbyhorses, the colonized minds of most Sri Lankans, including her own children, and she would have continued in this vein if Jane-Nona had not come out of the kitchen, bearing the drinks tray.

"*Ah.*" Uncle Lucky took the tray from her. "It's time for my arrack and ginger beer. Let's go out into the courtyard."

They were meeting together again to discuss the party and, once they were all seated, Aunty Bundle began with enthusiasm, having forgotten her previous annoyance. "Girls, girls, I've had a brilliant idea. Last night, at Chloe Coomaraswamy's dinner, she had the most wonderful hopper woman. I have never tasted hoppers like that, so light and crisp and delicious. We could hire her to do hoppers for your birthday." Aunty Bundle had a great fondness for these bowl-shaped crepes.

"But what about godamba rotis?" Mala asked, as they were her particular favorite, "I thought we were getting a godamba man to set his cart up in the courtyard."

"We will do both hoppers and godamba rotis," Aunty Bundle declared.

They all nodded. This sounded like a wonderful idea.

"And what about dessert, Amma?" Selvi asked. "My friend Otara knows this lady who makes lovely meringue and chocolate cream puddings."

They agreed they would consider that for dessert. But there would also be two birthday cakes from Perera and Sons and lots of trifles and soufflés and puddings. Then the discussion moved on to the number of guests. Aunty Bundle had brought a pad of paper and pen with her and they began to make a list. After they had put down their numerous relatives and family friends, the girls each gave the names of students in their class they wanted to invite. All the boys coming to the party would be relatives, or sons of family friends. When they were done, Aunty Bundle turned to Amrith. "And how about you, son? Any boys from your drama society?"

He shifted uncomfortably. "*Um* . . . no, Aunty."

"Well, that's alright, dear." She went back to the guest list, a look of concern in her eyes.

As Aunty Bundle began to read the list, which totaled about a hundred, Amrith felt depressed that not a single person on it was his friend or relative.

# 7

# Amrith Has a Surprise

~~~~~~~
~~~~~~~

Despite having a car and a driver, Uncle Lucky liked to walk in Fort when going about his business. "A chance to keep in touch with the common man," he called it. "A chance to remember where I came from."

One morning, he took Amrith with him to the bank. Their walk led them through the colonnaded arcade that ran in front of Cargil's Department Store.

The arcade was congested. Peons hurried about, carrying large manila envelopes, files, tiffin carriers; businessmen in ties strolled by on an early lunch; Cinnamon Gardens ladies bustled along, followed by servants staggering under the weight of parcels; beggars with all manner of deformities held out their palms, faces twisted in entreaty. There were hawkers on either side of the arcade forcing an even narrower passage for the pedestrians. From vivid pink or blue plastic sheets spread on the ground, they sold Bombay film posters, cassettes, socks, underpants, dress shirts in their crinkly wrapping, handbags, incense, wind-up toys from China, and knickknacks.

Amrith had to pay attention to where he was going, and he hurried to keep up with Uncle Lucky, who strode along as if there was no one in his way.

So, by the time Amrith was aware of the man and boy, he had already passed them and found himself turning to look at them. They were wearing shorts, which immediately marked them as foreigners, Sri Lankan foreigners in this case. They had stopped, or rather the boy, who appeared about Amrith's age but was much taller, had made the man stop so they could look at some garishly painted wooden elephants. Amrith, who still walked on even as he looked back, bumped right into Uncle Lucky. He, too, had come to a standstill and was staring at the man and boy.

The foreigners had lost interest in the elephants. They continued on and were immediately lost in the swell of pedestrians.

"Oh, *ah*," Uncle Lucky pressed Amrith's shoulder, not taking his eyes off the crowd. "Amrith, just . . . stand over there by the entrance to Cargil's. A client . . . I must go."

With that, Uncle Lucky, in a manner that was so uncharacteristic of him, practically ran after the foreigners.

It was some time before he came back. He was sweating. "A client, from Singapore. Good thing I caught him, as he was on his way to my office." Uncle Lucky took out his handkerchief and wiped his brow. "Come," he said, gesturing towards the cool interior of Cargil's, "let's go and have a glass of passion fruit cordial."

Amrith followed him, puzzled by Uncle Lucky's strange behavior, the agitated look on his face.

They were standing by the refreshment counter, sipping their drinks through straws, when, without any preamble, Uncle Lucky said, "Yes-yes, you children are very blessed not to be poor like I was at your age."

Uncle Lucky's teenage years – they had risen to mythical status in his narration of the terrible poverty he and his mother had endured after his father died. More marvelous than the martyrdoms of Aunty Bundle's saints. How poor Uncle Lucky, at the tender age of fifteen, had to give up his schooling, his dream of being an engineer, and go out to work. The sheer luxury of one egg a week; the eating of every unwanted part of a cow; the fact that he did not taste chicken until he was nineteen years old; the one office shirt, which was washed every evening by his mother, and which, during the monsoon, he sometimes wore damp to work the next day. The list was endless, but the ultimate goal of this litany was always the same – a reminder to the children of how fortunate they were to have a father like him; how very lucky they were to have an Uncle Lucky.

So, Amrith waited for the recital with a mental rolling of his eyes. Instead, Uncle Lucky stared into the distance for a while. "My father, you know, had quite a decent civil service job. We should not have been so poor after his death. He had this brother, you see. Their parents had left them a piece of land in Jaffna, to be equally divided, but the

brother simply took it for himself. After all, it made sense –
he was the one living up there in Jaffna and my father was
here in Colombo. But my father would not see it that way.
He took his own brother to court. *Ttttch,* sadly not an
uncommon practice among our Sri Lankans. People say
family-family, but the courts are jam-packed with children
suing parents, brothers suing sisters, sisters suing brothers.
Disgusting. And all the disputes are over dowry and property.
That's why I'm not giving a dowry to my girls. And you too,
no property. I'll give you all a good foreign university education, but that's that. Much better than this dowry rubbish."

Uncle Lucky was on yet another familiar tangent. He
cut himself short. "Anyway, this court case dragged on for
years and years. My father lost-lost-lost, but he simply
would not give up. All our money was siphoned off to pay
dishonest lawyers. My father was in debt and still continued this dispute. In the end, the pressure got to him. He
had a heart attack. He was my age, forty-four, can you
imagine?" Uncle Lucky took a long slurp through his straw.
"Years later, when I was more on my feet, I went to see this
piece of land that had ruined my father, my mother, our
life." He shook his head. "You won't believe it. Nothing! A
piece of dry scrubland, the worst lime-filled sandy soil, a few
thorny shrubs, and some palmyra trees. This was the thing
my father had destroyed his life over?" He looked hard at
Amrith. "Families hold on to things for too long, nurse
grievances until they corrode their hearts and ruin their
lives. How much better it is to forgive old wrongs, to let

things go. It frees you up to get on with your life. My father should have just let his brother have that damn land."

When they left Cargil's and continued on towards the bank, Amrith found himself looking at Uncle Lucky. He wondered why he had kept this story from them all these years. And why had he chosen to tell Amrith now? For it was clear to him that the lesson about families forgetting old wrongs and not nursing grievances was, in some way, directed at him.

~~~~~

The next morning, Amrith was at work on his typing exercises when the foreign man he had seen in the arcade came into the office.

Miss Rani went to greet the stranger, her countenance questioning but deferential. The man said a few words to her and she ushered him towards Uncle Lucky's office. Amrith had a better chance to look at the foreigner. He was only Amrith's height, about five feet, six inches, with a bony chest, skinny arms and legs, knobby knees visible below his shorts. The man's batik shirt was open at the collar, exposing a wiry tuft of hair, and his Adam's apple bounced up and down as if in nervousness. His face was bony, with thin lips and a prominent forehead, made even more pronounced by his receding hairline. There was a look of petulance, of dissatisfaction, on his face.

After a discreet knock, Miss Rani opened the cubicle door. Amrith heard the rapid scraping of a chair as Uncle Lucky rose to his feet. There was a moment of silence, then a murmured greeting. Both men sat down. Miss Rani closed the door. People often came to see Uncle Lucky on business, sometimes foreigners, so Amrith did not think any more about it.

As he typed away, however, it came to him that something was not quite as it should be. He paused to move the carriage back into position and listened. The men were talking in fits and starts, with long silences and much clearing of throats.

After a while, the foreigner came out alone. As he started towards the entrance, he turned to look at Amrith. When their eyes met, his expression was irritated yet apprehensive. And suddenly a suspicion began to open up in Amrith's mind, fueled by Uncle Lucky's story yesterday about family grievances.

Uncle Lucky stepped out of his office and signaled to Amrith. His face was stern. As Amrith got up from his chair and approached him, his legs were trembling.

Uncle Lucky gestured to one of the stuffed leather chairs by his desk.

Amrith sat down.

Uncle Lucky went to stand at the window, looking onto Chatham Street. "The thing is, son," he said, turning to Amrith, "that man who came into my office. He's not a client from Singapore. He's your . . . your Canadian uncle. Your mother's brother."

Amrith gasped – not so much from surprise, but rather at this confirmation of what he had already suspected.

Uncle Lucky crossed the room and sat in the chair next to him. "Are you alright, son?"

Amrith nodded. His throat was dry. He swallowed. Outside on Chatham Street, he could hear the rushing of traffic, the blaring of horns, the singing of a beggar, concrete girders crashing into place on a construction site.

Uncle Lucky pressed his arm. "Your cousin, Niresh, did not know you existed. He did not even know his father had a sister. The first time he found out was yesterday, when I accidentally let the cat out of the bag. Niresh really wants to meet you. He has been pestering-pestering-pestering his father. Your uncle, because of his animosity towards your mother, is not very keen for this meeting. But he has finally given in. They are staying at the Mount Lavinia Hotel. We are to visit them tomorrow, before lunch."

Amrith could not look at Uncle Lucky. There was such a welling up of emotion in him, he was frightened he would start to cry.

That afternoon, as he lay on his bed, Amrith contemplated this momentous turn of events. His uncle and cousin from Canada were here. Tomorrow afternoon, by now, he would have met them.

His mother had told him about these Canadian relatives, but she had not mentioned the bitter conflict with her brother. After his mother's funeral, Aunty Bundle went to great effort and expense to track down his uncle. She had made numerous calls to Sri Lankans in Canada and finally secured an address for him. She had sent a telegram, followed by an express-post letter, telling him about his sister's death, that Amrith was living with them. She had asked nothing of him; she merely wanted to give him a chance to connect with his nephew, to put an end to past hostilities. His uncle had never called, never written. Amrith remembered the look of sadness and anger on Aunty Bundle's face when she got a letter from her contact in Canada, confirming that his uncle had, indeed, received the dispatches.

At that time, Amrith was still in shock from his parents' death and he felt little emotion about the rejection. In fact, he was not very surprised by it. His father's family had already disowned him, and he had even been prevented from attending his father's funeral at the family ancestral home, in Kurunegela. His father had been expected to marry for wealth and provide dowries for his sisters. By marrying his mother, who came with nothing, he had brought financial hardship to his family and forced his sisters into a life of spinsterhood. These relatives bore a great hatred towards his son.

Amrith went to his chest of drawers, took out the leather-bound photo album, and turned the pages to the photograph of his mother as an adult. As he gazed at it, he found himself thinking of how, when he was twelve, Aunty Bundle and Uncle Lucky had taken him to lunch in the Rainbow Room at the Grand Oriental Hotel. Once they had ordered, Uncle Lucky had leaned forward in his chair, his hands clasped on the linen tablecloth, and said, "Amrith, I do not believe in our Sri Lankan habit of *shoo-shoo-boo-boo.* Hiding things."

And so Amrith had been told the details of his mother's family life and the cause of her bitter conflict with her brother.

His grandmother had been a sickly and gentle woman who had died not long after his mother was born. His grandfather, a prominent lawyer, had been a terror in court and at home. The only one exempt from his cruelty was his son, Mervin. From the beginning, he adored his boy and spared him nothing. In contrast, he despised his daughter. He nicknamed her loris, after that thin lizard with a spindly body, large head, and bulging-out eyes. Mervin, too, was unkind to his sister. He ordered her around like a servant and, if she refused his slightest wish, he would tell his father. Then his sister would be called to the study and his father would beat her with his belt.

A year after Amrith's uncle had gone to study law in England, his grandfather developed an eye disease that would soon make him blind. The old man had expected his daughter would take care of him but, by then, she had met Amrith's father. When she ran away and got married, his grandfather promptly disowned her. He called on his son to look after him, asking him to return and complete his studies in Sri Lanka. But his son never responded to his pleas. It was too much for the old man. His blood pressure rose and, one day, a servant found him dead in his study. Only then did his son come back to Sri Lanka. He went around telling everyone that his sister had killed their father with her selfishness and he forbade her to attend the funeral. He made a big show of sorrow at the funeral but, all the while, he had hired a matchmaker to find him a bride. He met his future wife, Therese, the day after he buried his father. She was from Kalutara gentry, but her family had fallen on hard times and was so poor they lived in the back room of a relative's house. She was a very beautiful woman. Within a week, his uncle had married her and they went back to England. Later, they moved to Canada.

When Amrith had heard all this, he felt as if the ground had opened up under him and he was falling through darkness, helpless in the face of this past, about which he could do nothing.

Now that very same darkness engulfed him. He put away the album and went to lie on his bed, turned on a side, his legs drawn up to his chest.

≈≈≈≈
≈≈≈≈

Uncle Lucky, wanting to give Amrith some time to take in the news, was only going to tell the rest of the family when they sat out in the courtyard before dinner.

That evening, while Amrith played a game of Chinese Checkers with the sisters, he listened to the voices of the adults at the other end of the courtyard. He felt like there was a lump of ice in his chest that sent little rivulets of coldness up and down his arms and legs. He was dreading this announcement, as if something shameful about himself was going to be revealed. He was particularly dreading Aunty Bundle's reaction.

"Amrith," Selvi nudged him, "how long are you going to stare at that board, men?"

"Akka, let him take his time," Mala said, coming to Amrith's defense. "What is your big hurry?"

Amrith had not realized it was his turn. He moved a piece without much thought.

Selvi, with a triumphant "Lovely," took three of his pieces.

He barely noticed for, at that moment, Uncle Lucky said something and Aunty Bundle exclaimed as if she had been stung.

The girls straightened up from their Checkers game and looked across the courtyard.

Uncle Lucky continued on in a steady murmur.

"Mervin is here, from Canada?" Aunty Bundle cried incredulously.

Mala and Selvi knew about his Canadian relatives and they stared at Amrith.

"Your uncle is here?" Selvi demanded.

Amrith looked away.

Selvi jumped to her feet and hurried across the court-yard, ignoring Mala calling her to come back . . . that it was none of their business. Mala went after her sister. Despite her reticence, she, too, was eager to know more about this news.

Amrith felt he had no choice but to join the rest of the family. He got up reluctantly and went over to them.

"Appa, Amrith's uncle is here?" Selvi stood beside his chair.

Uncle Lucky nodded. "His cousin, too. We are to meet them tomorrow."

The girls drew in their breath.

Amrith had come up to them and he could feel Aunty Bundle's gaze. He lifted his eyes to her. She looked stricken and, seeing the pain in her eyes, a corresponding anguish began to open up in him.

Mala had seen her mother's and Amrith's suffering, but Selvi, oblivious to it, began to ply Uncle Lucky with questions. Amrith slipped away to his room.

A few minutes later, Selvi barged in without knocking, followed by a reluctant Mala.

He was at his almirah, putting away a pile of clean clothes that Jane-Nona had left on a chair. He did not look around.

"My God, Amrith, what a thing, *nah*." Selvi threw herself on his bed.

Mala sat beside her sister. "Amrith, are you alright?"

"What did your cousin look like?" Selvi demanded.

"*Um* . . . I don't remember." Which was partially true. He recalled that his cousin had been very tall and perhaps dark-skinned, but that was all.

"Ca-na-da. Mala, what do you know about Canada?" Selvi asked.

Mala frowned. "It's cold there, akka, freezing."

"Yes-yes, we all know that. But what else? Do you think it's like America? Would they have malls and up-to-date films and music?"

"*Ttttch,* of course, akka. *Ah,* but I just remembered something!"

"What-what?"

"Anne Murray comes from Canada."

"Yes! And Anne of Green Gables, too."

But besides the two Annes, they were stumped when it came to Canada.

There was a knock on the door and Aunty Bundle came in. "Amrith, I want to speak to you. Alone." She had been crying, her eyes red.

"Come, akka, let's go," Mala whispered to Selvi, "I told you we should have left Amrith alone." They got off the bed. Selvi looked guilty, aware she had been insensitive.

Mala smiled at Amrith. "I'm sure your cousin will be very nice."

"Yes-yes," Selvi nodded, "I'm sure you'll really like him."

They left, closing the door softly behind them.

"Amrith," Aunty Bundle began, resting her hand on the bedpost. "You must go and meet your cousin tomorrow. But I . . . I don't want anything to do with your uncle and his family. Because of your mother. You understand, son, don't you? I couldn't stand to see him."

The return of his uncle had brought back the pain of his mother's death to Aunty Bundle. Looking at her tear-streaked face, he felt a bitter anger take hold. He turned away and stood, his hands clenched by his sides.

She was waiting for him to respond, but when he would not do so, she left with a sigh.

The moment she was gone, he breathed out and sat down on the bed. He put his head in his hands. "I hate her," he whispered between clenched teeth, "I just hate her."

That night, Amrith dreamt about his mother. It was a dream he often had. He was running along the road that led to the estate bungalow, in a panic. He raced through the gate, up the driveway, and around the side of the house. He rushed onto the veranda and then stopped, a terror taking hold. His mother's chair was empty. He had arrived too late. He had failed to save her from a terrible fate.

Amrith, as he always did, woke at this point with a gasp. A sense of menace was palpable all around him. Even after he had switched on the bedside lamp, his fear did not abate. The threat just withdrew beyond his door and lurked in the courtyard and side garden.

# 8

# The Canadian Cousin

~~~~~~~~
~~~~~~~~

Even before he met his relatives the next day, Amrith had already heard news about them. That morning, they were in the middle of breakfast when Aunt Wilhelmina hurried in after her game of tennis, crying, "Bun-dle, Bun-dle." She was dressed all in white, wearing linen slacks, a long-sleeved shirt, and a wide-brimmed straw hat – clothes that were ridiculously warm for sports, but that kept her European skin immaculate.

She saw them at the dining table and came up the steps.

"Bundle." She gestured towards the library, with a quick glance at Amrith. "Come-come, child, I have something I simply must tell you. I had a game this morning with Lady Rajapakse and you will not believe what I have learnt."

"We know, Aunt Wilhelmina." Aunty Bundle sighed. "Lucky met Mervin in Fort."

"Oh." She was a bit put out. Then she brightened up. "But, child-child, did you know that he is divorced?" She smiled, gratified by the looks on their faces. "Yes, for a very long time, it seems."

Amrith was shocked. Divorce was a very shameful thing. There were a few students in his school, like Peries, whose parents were separated and they never spoke of it, often pretending their parents were still married.

Aunt Wilhelmina sat down and, sipping a cup of tea Jane-Nona had placed before her, told them all she knew.

Mervin's wife, Therese, had left him when Niresh was eight years old. Physical and mental cruelty were the reasons cited for the divorce. Niresh's mother had remarried. A Canadian man, who ran a cattle farm in a place called Alberta. Evidently, the second marriage was not altogether successful, the man being a crude, bullying type. "Which," Aunt Wilhelmina said with a sniff, "was to be expected if one went off and married a farmer."

Aunt Wilhelmina now moved on to gossip about Niresh. He was sixteen years old. Although he currently lived with his father in a Toronto suburb, he had spent most of his youth in boarding schools.

Aunty Bundle shook her head, when she heard this. "That poor-poor boy," she murmured.

"Evidently, he's a handful." Aunt Wilhelmina raised her eyebrows. "Always in some trouble or other. He's been to three boarding schools and was asked to leave each of them."

When Aunt Wilhelmina was told that Amrith was to see his cousin this morning, she frowned. "I'd be careful.

Amrith is a very sweet, gentle boy. This Niresh could be a terrible influence on him."

The news that his cousin was truant like Suraj Wanigasekera only made Amrith more anxious.

"The question that interests me," Aunt Wilhelmina continued, "is *why* Mervin has returned, after all these years. I have known that blackguard since he was a boy and I am sure money is somehow involved." She narrowed her eyes. "I have put out some inquiries. Let us see what turns up."

～～～～
～～～～

Soma dropped Uncle Lucky and Amrith in front of the Mount Lavinia Hotel and went to park. Amrith stood looking at the imposing whitewashed facade, with its pillars and domes. All through his typing exercises there had been a cold lump in his stomach. Uncle Lucky took Amrith's arm and guided him towards the entrance. A guard in a solar-topee and a white coat swung open the brass-studded door and they entered into chaos.

The lobby was packed with German tourists checking out, their bags all over the floor. Deputy managers barked out orders; a dozen porters rushed back and forth from the lobby to the waiting bus in the courtyard. The Germans were loud and enormous, their faces florid, their teeth gleaming as they yelled to each other, threw back their heads and roared with laughter, harangued the terrified staff behind the reception desk about their bills. Uncle Lucky gripped Amrith's arm. They plunged into the Germans and wedged their way past the large bodies, avoiding tripping over the bags or being hit in the face by the tourists' broad gestures.

To the side of the lobby was a lounge area, with chairs and settees around coffee tables. His uncle rose from one of the chairs and held up his hand to get their attention.

As they went across to him, Amrith kept his eyes lowered, even more nervous than before.

When they reached his relative, Uncle Lucky gently pushed him forward. "Amrith, this is your Uncle Mervin."

He held out his hand and his uncle took it limply. He glanced up and saw a forced smile on his face.

They sat down.

His uncle looked around, worried. "Niresh should be here soon."

Uncle Lucky cleared his throat. He asked Amrith's uncle how long they were going to be here, where they planned to go, what they had seen so far. Mervin answered, prolonging his responses to prevent any pauses.

As the adults talked, Amrith began to feel strange, almost surreal, to be seated here in front of a relative of his. He gazed at his uncle, searching his face for any resemblance to his mother. There was none, and he did not know if he was glad of this or not.

The two men finally became silent, having exhausted all topics of conversation.

His uncle looked around again, frowning. He signaled to the Guest Relations Officer, who was by the reception desk. She came over to them.

"You haven't seen my son, have you?"

"Oh, yes, Mr. Fonseka, he's in the pool."

"In the pool?" His uncle struggled to hide his surprise. "Thank you."

She nodded and walked away, an amused smile on her face. His cousin appeared to be notorious here.

"I . . . I don't understand what he's doing in the pool." His uncle stood up. "I told him you all were coming today. Excuse me."

"Amrith," Uncle Lucky said, indicating for him to get up, "why don't you go with your uncle and meet your cousin?"

His uncle was rather discomfited by this, but he said, "Yes, of course."

Amrith rose shakily to his feet. His uncle led the way across the foyer and he followed, surreptitiously rubbing his sweaty palms against his jeans.

They were silent as they climbed the red-carpeted stairs. Finally his uncle asked gruffly, "And what grade are you in?"

"*Um . . . um . . .* grade nine." Amrith was about to add "Uncle," like he would have done as a sign of respect to any older man, but the word froze in his mouth.

"So you are doing your O levels next year?"

Amrith nodded, so conscious of being unable to say "Uncle" that he felt awkward speaking at all.

"And what do you plan to study for your A levels? Arts or Sciences?"

"*Um . . . um . . .* Arts."

His uncle glanced at him and Amrith, suddenly afraid that he might be considered rude, blurted out, "Uncle."

The moment he said it, a mixture of emotions flitted over his uncle's face. He looked away.

They had come out on an elevated terrace, from which there was a sweeping view of the sea below. A hem of gleaming beach curved for miles along the Colombo bay, ending at the office towers of the Fort area. It had rained this morning and there were puddles of water on the terrace, shimmering in the noonday sun. All the objects on the terrace had devoured their own shadows and their colors were stark, without any grace of shade – the brassy pink of the potted bougainvilleas, the harsh yellow of the patio umbrellas, the bloated whiteness of the plastic lounging chairs.

In the pool, a boy was swimming up and down in an uncoordinated manner, splashing lots of water about as he did the freestyle, his head shooting up to take loud gasps of air.

His uncle went to the edge of the pool. "Niresh, Niresh." He had to repeat the name a few times more before the boy heard him.

Niresh spun around and stood up, all at the same time, the water pouring down his face, his mouth opening and shutting like a fish.

"Your cousin is here." His uncle sounded both irritated and embarrassed.

Niresh looked at Amrith. His eyes grew wide. "Fuck!" he cried, his mouth gaping open in dismay. "What time is it?" He glanced over at the clock on the wall and then thrashed through the water to them. He pulled himself out of the pool, scattering a shower of drops like a dog. His cousin was well over six feet, with gangly heavy limbs, dark hairless skin that had a golden undertone, a wide floppy mouth that hung open now as he struggled to catch his breath.

When he was sufficiently composed, he turned to his father, his hands on his hips. "Man, what's your problem?" he boomed. "You told me they were coming at one o'clock."

His uncle's face grew red with wrath. "Don't call me man. And I did not tell you one o'clock. I said twelve o'clock."

"The hell you did. Why would I be in the damn pool, if I knew Amrith was coming?"

Niresh used his name as if he already knew him. Amrith, who had been intimidated from the moment his cousin had cried out "fuck," saw now that there was a theatricality to Niresh's stance. He had his hands on his hips and his voice was raised louder than necessary. This was for Amrith's benefit.

"But I told you twelve o'clock, Niresh," his uncle insisted. "Don't talk nonsense."

"You don't talk nonsense, man. You're going senile."

His uncle was enraged. Yet his son was taller and stronger than him and, as if to make this point, Niresh stood close to his father, towering over him.

"I don't have time for this nonsense," his uncle said, stepping back. "Wipe yourself off. Put on a shirt." He stalked away with as much dignity as he could.

Niresh turned to Amrith, winked, and grinned. "What do you get when you cross a lemon with a cat?" He indicated towards the retreating figure of his father. "A sourpuss."

Amrith gave a surprised giggle, and his cousin threw his head back and laughed at his own joke.

Niresh held out a wet hand. "It's really great to meet you."

Amrith offered his hand and his cousin gave it such a hearty squeeze that he winced.

Niresh took up his towel. "Sorry about the mix-up." He grinned at him wickedly. "My fault. I got the time wrong."

Amrith was staggered at how well his cousin had faked outrage and innocence.

Niresh rubbed his head vigorously for a few moments, flung his towel on a lounge chair, and put on a shirt. His hair, which came down to the nape of his neck and covered his ears, stood out at all angles. "Come on, let's walk around a bit."

Niresh led the way along the balustrade that bordered the terrace. "So," he said, after a few moments, "did you even know I existed?"

Amrith nodded.

"Well, I had no idea about you. And *we* know who's to blame for that." He grimaced ruefully at Amrith. By doing so, he both acknowledged and, at the same time, laid aside what was really a tragic omission in both their lives.

Niresh stopped at the corner pedestal of the balustrade. He reached into his shirt pocket and drew out a pack of cigarettes. He offered one to Amrith, who quickly shook his head.

Amrith tried not to stare as his cousin, right out here where anyone could see, lit a cigarette. Even the worst boy in his school would not dare to smoke so publicly.

"So, if a baby was aborted in Czechoslovakia, what would that baby be?" He waited as Amrith dutifully shook his head. "A canceled Czech."

Amrith did not think it was that funny, but he grinned nonetheless and his cousin laughed.

They began to talk, or rather, Niresh questioned him about Colombo and Amrith answered, pointing out various landmarks in the distance, showing him the bottom of their street and Kinross Beach, where they often went swimming.

Niresh asked him about the Manuel-Pillais. He seemed intrigued by Uncle Lucky's aquarium, but when Amrith told him that Aunty Bundle was an interior decorator for an architect who specialized in buildings that drew on ancient Sri Lankan architecture, his eyes grew wide. He asked Amrith numerous questions about her work and the buildings Lucien Lindamulagé designed. He wanted to know exactly what constituted a Sri Lankan style of architecture, and Amrith told him about the courtyards and mada midulas, which were interior gardens around which the houses were sometimes built. He also told him about specific wood carvings on pillars and doorways and the latticework above windows.

His cousin also wanted to know about Selvi and Mala – how old they were and if they had boyfriends. When Amrith explained that Aunty Bundle and Uncle Lucky did not want any of them to date until they were past eighteen, Niresh shook his head in amazement and said that was "far out."

As they talked, the high monsoon waves crashed against the rocks below them. Two boys with straw hats were fishing from a large flat boulder that jutted out into the sea.

Amrith noticed that Niresh had begun to sweat pro-fusely, stains appearing under his arms and on his back, moisture gathering on his forehead and chin and upper lip. Niresh was not used to their tropical climate. He kept rubbing his face with his sleeve, which grew increasingly soggy. Finally, Amrith took out a handkerchief and offered it to him. Niresh looked at the handkerchief, not sure what he should do with it, but when Amrith gestured towards his face, Niresh grinned in thanks and wiped himself with it.

Amrith was telling Niresh about his school – whose system of houses and prefects and addressing one another by last names seemed to fascinate Niresh, who said it was like something out of an old-time British movie – when he heard his name being called. He turned to see Uncle Lucky walking towards them. He glanced at his watch, amazed at how quickly time had passed.

Niresh hurriedly stubbed out his cigarette and flung it over the balustrade to the beach below.

"Son," Uncle Lucky said, smiling, "it's time to go home for lunch."

"You're leaving so soon?" Niresh's jaw dropped in disappointment. "Can't Amrith stay for lunch?"

Uncle Lucky struggled with this. The invitation had not come from Niresh's father. "I'm afraid not. Food has already been prepared for Amrith at home and –"

"Hold on a sec. I'll ask my dad."

Without waiting for Uncle Lucky's response, Niresh ran across the terrace and down the corridor.

Uncle Lucky turned to Amrith. "So you and your cousin are getting on well?"

Amrith nodded. He was delighted at how comfortable he was with Niresh, as if they had always known each other.

"Good-good." Uncle Lucky smiled. "It was the right thing to meet him."

Niresh came back in a surprisingly short time. He smiled broadly. "My dad said Amrith could stay."

Uncle Lucky seemed a little taken aback that Niresh's father had agreed to this, but he nodded and told Amrith he would pick him up at five o'clock.

The moment he left, they grinned at each other and Niresh cried, "Yeah! This is great!" In his delight, he thumped Amrith on the shoulders so hard he nearly coughed.

Niresh went to change and, when he came back, he led Amrith to lunch. They entered a large ballroom with mirrors on the wall, the lamp brackets and ceiling cornices decorated with gilt. There was a buffet table set up at one end, covered with white tablecloths and piled with both Sri Lankan and Western food. Another table, a little distance away, had the desserts.

The room was crowded with tourists lining up to fill their plates, or sitting at the round tables and eating. His uncle was alone at a table.

Niresh led the way towards his father. When his uncle saw Amrith, he looked astonished.

"Hey, Dad," Niresh said, as they came up to the table, "Amrith's staying for lunch."

He was not asking his father's permission, he was telling him. His tone was casually contemptuous, as if his father's consent did not count at all. Without waiting for a response, Niresh led Amrith towards the buffet table.

As they stood in line with their plates, Amrith expected his cousin to say something about his lie but, instead, he treated Amrith to more jokes – What do you get when you cross a stripper with a banana? A self-peeling banana. What's the difference between in-laws and outlaws? Outlaws are wanted. Why did the chicken cross the road twice? Because it was a double-crosser.

None of the jokes were very funny, but Niresh told them with such an eagerness to please that Amrith had to respond with dutiful laughter. It was clear to him that Niresh was keen to impress him, to win his affection. From the first moment of their meeting, his cousin had set out determinedly to build a relationship between them. Amrith had never been courted in this way by anybody, and it was especially flattering because Niresh was two years older than him.

By the time they were sitting down to eat, at a table across the room from his uncle's, Amrith had forgiven Niresh his lie.

From what he knew of his uncle's cruelty to his mother, Amrith guessed that his uncle had been harsh to his son when he was younger. The relish with which Niresh wielded his power over his father made Amrith suspect it was new-found; an ascendancy that had come to his cousin as he grew taller and stronger than his father. Amrith was glad of this shift of power. It was his uncle's just due for the unhappiness he had caused in so many lives.

〰〰〰

That afternoon, Niresh confessed to Amrith a burning desire he had since coming to Sri Lanka – he wanted to drive one of those three-wheeled, scooterlike, open-sided trishaw taxis that were parked outside the hotel gates. He did not speak Sinhalese and he wanted Amrith to translate for him.

At first, the trishaw drivers were amused at the proposition but, when they saw that Niresh was serious, they eyed him with suspicion. The youngest among them, a boy about eighteen, wanted to know if his cousin had driven before. Niresh produced a card with his photograph on it, which he held out to them, saying it was his driver's license. The writing was in English and they could not read it. Amrith could. The laminated card was for membership at a gym. His cousin held his gaze intently and Amrith had no choice but to confirm for the trishaw men that it was, indeed, a driver's license.

The youngest driver agreed for the princely sum of three hundred rupees. Niresh was unfazed. He drew out a thick wad of hundred-rupee bills from his wallet and counted three. Amrith watched him in awe. He did not even own a wallet.

Once the trishaw driver had pocketed the money, he handed over the keys. With a grin of utter delight, Niresh took his place in the driver's seat. He looked like a giant in a Lilliputian conveyance, his long legs sticking out beyond the edges of the trishaw, his head brushing the roof.

Niresh started the motor and shouted above its noise for Amrith to hop in. He could not refuse as it would raise the suspicions of the owner. He reluctantly took his place in the backseat. The young driver was showing Niresh the controls, but his cousin seemed to barely listen. He was revving the engine, anxious to be on his way.

Finally the driver stepped aside, Niresh revved the engine to its utmost and, with a war cry, they took off, the trishaw weaving drunkenly from side to side. After a few moments, Niresh managed to straighten the front wheel and they picked up speed, leaving the trishaw men behind. Amrith hung on grimly to the bars that separated the back from the driver's seat.

His cousin was beside himself. He kept whooping *yee-ha, yee-ha* over and over again, as if he were a cowboy riding a horse. He threw back his head and roared in delight, his hair standing up on end in the breeze.

After some time, Amrith loosened his grip on the bars. He began to enjoy the adventure, to look out at the passing scenery. Then they rounded a corner and, ahead of them, they saw a brood of chickens in the middle of the road. Niresh cried out as the chickens squawked and fluttered into the air. He swerved to avoid the birds and the trishaw tipped madly. It careened off the road and rushed towards a thicket of bushes. Amrith and Niresh yelled in fear and, the next moment, the trishaw plowed right into the foliage and wedged itself between two branches, its wheels growling in the dirt.

"Fuck, fuck, fuck," Niresh bellowed. He switched the motor off and thumped the steering wheel, as if the vehicle were at fault.

Amrith got out. His legs were wobbly and he held on to the side of the trishaw for a moment.

They crept out from under the foliage and stood on the road.

Amrith could taste grit in his mouth. His cousin's face was covered in dust and there were leaves and twigs in his hair. Niresh was looking at him too. They began to giggle. Soon they were laughing hysterically, clutching on to each other.

The owner arrived a few minutes later, driven by a gray-haired trishaw driver. When he saw his vehicle in the bushes, he hopped up and down in anguish, as if he were stepping on hot coals. The older man was more sanguine. He pushed the trishaw out of the thicket, walked around and pointed out that there were just a few scratches on it. He got the young driver to start the vehicle. It worked fine. The older man chided him for being foolish, for jeopardizing his livelihood and the welfare of his family for a few hundred rupees.

Amrith and Niresh walked back to the hotel. They had their arms around each other's shoulders and, every so often, they broke apart to recount a moment in their adventure and laugh over it.

Amrith had never felt so alive.

# 9

## Niresh's
## "Terrible Influence"

~~~~~~~~~~
~~~~~~~~~~

When Amrith got home that evening and was in his bedroom untying his shoelaces, the girls charged in.

Selvi threw herself on the bed. "So-so, tell-tell."

"Yes, Amrith, how was it?" Mala rested a hand on his shoulder. "Did you like him?"

"What did he look like?" Selvi demanded.

"A boy." He kicked off his shoes.

Selvi rolled her eyes. "But is he tall or short, fat or thin, fair or dark?"

"Tall, thin, dark." He began to remove his socks. Some of his cousin's wickedness had brushed off on him.

"*Ttttch,* don't be so stubborn, Amrith. Tell, will you?" Selvi had no doubt promised her friends a full account.

"Why are you so keen to know? Are you looking for a foreign boyfriend?"

"*Huh,*" Selvi sniffed. "I see your cousin is already a terrible influence on you."

Amrith sauntered into his bathroom, whistling, and shut the door after him.

Selvi did not give up that easily. When they were at dinner, she asked her father what Niresh looked like.

"He needs a good haircut." Uncle Lucky was teasing his daughter.

"He has long hair!" Mala exclaimed.

"Looks like a real ragamuffin," Uncle Lucky continued. "Fringe like a girl's, hair over his ears, which of course means he can't hear properly."

"You mean," Selvi gasped, "he has a haircut like Shaun Cassidy?"

"I have no idea who you are talking about." Though, of course, Uncle Lucky knew. Like all of them, he had heard "Da Do Ron Ron" a few too many times.

The sisters looked at each other in awe. "Mala," Selvi said, in a hushed tone, "Amrith's cousin has a haircut like Shaun Cassidy."

Mala shook her head, impressed.

~~~~~

Later that evening, Amrith stood in front of his almirah mirror, the closed copy of *Othello* in his hand. He had intended to go over his part but, with rehearsals still two weeks away, he could not summon the desire to do so. Instead, he was thinking about his cousin's haircut. The strict dress code at Amrith's school forced students to wear their hair very short. He was hoping that, by the end of the holidays, his hair would be long enough to blow-dry into a more fashionable style.

Amrith found himself thinking of the way Niresh had leaned on the balustrade, drawing on his cigarette and exhaling between slightly parted lips, with the panache of those men in the cigarette ads that play before a film. Despite Niresh's silly jokes, an aura of glamor hung around him.

A knock on his bedroom door brought him out of his thoughts. It was Jane-Nona. There was a telephone call from a boy with a foreign accent. Amrith ran across the courtyard to take it in the living room.

"Hey," Niresh said, when Amrith picked up the receiver, "what are you doing?"

"*Um*, nothing much," Amrith replied, feeling a great happiness take hold. "I was just in my room." He heard the receiver being lifted in the library, the sound of breathing. The girls were eavesdropping.

"Hi? You still there?" Niresh asked.

"Yes . . . *um* . . . someone's picked up the extension." He called out, "I'm on the phone."

"Oh, Amrith, hello, it's me, Selvi. I didn't realize you were on the phone." But she didn't put the receiver down.

"Excuse me, Niresh." Amrith stormed out of the living room into the library and glared at the girls. They grinned back. He snatched the phone from them, slammed the receiver down, and returned to the living room.

"Sorry, it's . . . *um* . . . my sisters," he said to Niresh.

"They were listening in?" Niresh had laughter in his voice.

"Yes, they were." Amrith smiled.

"Why? I guess they want to know about your cousin from abroad."

"Oh, yes, they've been asking all sorts of questions."

"Like?"

"How you looked, whether you were tall or short, fat or thin, fair or dark."

"What did you say?"

"Tall, thin, dark."

Niresh chortled. "Hey, get your sisters to write out a list of questions and we'll go through them. It'll be a gas."

"Sure."

"So, *uh,* what are you doing tomorrow afternoon?" Niresh asked.

"Nothing," Amrith replied.

"Do you want to hang out here?"

Amrith went to get permission from Aunty Bundle and Uncle Lucky, who were in the courtyard. The girls heard him leave the living room and they came out to discover what had happened. He ignored them and went back to tell Niresh he could come.

~~~~~
~~~~~

When Amrith entered the foyer of the Mount Lavinia Hotel the next afternoon, his cousin was waiting for him. They stood grinning with goodwill. "I'm glad you could make it," Niresh said, as they shook hands.

"Yes, me too. I brought the list." Amrith had wickedly pretended that he could not remember anything Selvi wanted him to ask and so, in frustration, Selvi, along with Mala, had agreed to make a list.

Niresh laughed. "Well, let's have a look," he said.

They sat in the lounge.

His cousin read the first question out loud. *"Do you go to a school that has both boys and girls in it?"* He frowned, puzzled. "Why would they ask? Of course I go to school with guys and girls. You don't?"

Amrith shook his head and explained that the schools were single sex.

"Wow, so, like, how do guys meet chicks?"

"*Um* . . . you can join an association, and then you get to do things with similar associations from girls' schools."

Niresh continued to read. "*Have you seen* A Little Romance? Shit, no. I wouldn't see such mushy crap. *What music do you like?* You guys heard of Ozzy Osbourne or Motley Crew?"

Amrith shook his head.

"Who do you guys listen to?"

"Olivia Newton-John, the Bee Gees, Sheena Easton, Shaun Cassidy."

"Gag! You're kidding me! *Do you have a girlfriend?* Not one, many. I like to keep my options open." Niresh grinned. "Hey, are your sisters home? Let's call and I can talk to them direct."

He took Amrith to his room, which was a mess – clothes strewn everywhere, a suitcase open on the floor.

Amrith dialed their number. Jane-Nona answered and he told her he wanted to speak to Selvi or Mala.

"Amrith?" Selvi came on the line, a little out of breath.

"Oh, hi, someone wants to talk to you." He handed the phone to Niresh.

His cousin beckoned him to come close. "Hi, this is Niresh."

A silence. "Oh, hello."

"So, I got your questions and I thought I'd call in person and answer them."

"Just a minute."

They heard a hurried conference between the sisters, Mala telling her to put down the phone, not to talk with a strange boy, Selvi saying he was not a stranger. Amrith and Niresh giggled.

"Hello." Selvi was back. "Sorry about that."

"So do you want to know my answers?"

"If you'd like to give them."

Amrith was surprised by Selvi's cool.

"But first, I'd like to ask you a question," Niresh said.

"Yes?"

"Are you tall or short, fat or thin, fair or dark?"

The boys fell back on the bed, killing themselves with laughter.

Finally, Niresh sobered down enough to pick up the receiver again. "So are you?"

"What?"

"Tall or short, fat or thin, fair or dark?"

"Can I speak to my brother?"

"Sure." He handed the receiver to Amrith.

"Amrith, I'm going to tell Amma."

"Tell her what?" he demanded.

"That you got your cousin to call and make fun of me."

"But you asked the questions and so he is answering now."

"You wait and see." With that, she banged the phone down.

They laughed and shook their heads.

"So why do your sisters want to know all this?" Niresh asked.

"Because . . . I guess . . . you're from abroad."

"And?"

Amrith paused, not sure how to explain the glamor of "abroad." "And . . . I suppose you get to see all the newest films and television programs, and we have to wait years for them to come out here. We only saw *Saturday Night Fever* this year."

"You're kidding me! That film came out in 1977 – three years ago."

"And," Amrith continued, "you get to listen to whatever music you want. I mean, we can't just go out and buy a record that we read about in the newspapers, because the government here restricts the importing of foreign things. We have to wait until my uncle or aunt goes abroad to get it, or buy it secondhand at an embassy sale."

"So, Canada is really cool to you guys?"

"Yes, I suppose it is cool."

Niresh nodded, taking this in. Then he stood up. "Hey, how about a walk on the beach?"

They went out into the hotel corridor and headed towards the terrace.

"Yeah," Niresh said, "Canada is great. As long as you're not some freak or nerd in school." He glanced quickly at Amrith, then his chest expanded slightly. "My close buddies – I've got three, Tommy, Dave, and Matt – we're on the football team and we're really tight."

He told Amrith about all the things he did with his buddies – going to movies and making out with chicks, hanging out at the mall, trying to get into clubs with fake IDs. The four of them often cruised around Markham, the suburb in which they lived, in Dave's car, causing havoc. Niresh thought this was the coolest thing. They would steal people's flowers in the summer, smash pumpkins at Halloween, remove the bulbs from outdoor Christmas lights. He told Amrith that he was having such a good time that he had not even wanted to visit Sri Lanka. He had planned to attend football camp with his buddies, but his father had forced him to come here instead.

Stories like Niresh's would have usually intimidated Amrith, but all the while his cousin talked, he had his arm around Amrith's shoulder, and he felt curiously included in Niresh's gang of friends.

Soon they were out on the terrace. As they started to cross it, a voice cried out, "Niresh, Niresh, come here, you bugger."

Amrith turned to see his uncle sitting in the shade of an awning with a group of Sri Lankan men.

"Fuck," Niresh muttered, under his breath. "Why?" he called back, not moving.

"Just get over here when I call you," his uncle bellowed.

Niresh began to walk over and Amrith followed reluctantly. Despite an appearance of civility, Amrith was aware that his uncle did not like him. His uncle's dislike was so strong, it blotted out Amrith's own emotions and, besides an awkwardness, he could not tell what he felt towards his uncle.

As they drew near, Amrith saw that there were two bottles of arrack on the table. One of them was already empty and it was barely four o'clock in the afternoon. His uncle's eyes were red. The other men looked drunk, too.

Niresh stopped a few yards away. "What do you want?"

"How dare you talk to me like that," his uncle snarled. His glance slid to Amrith and then away.

Niresh muttered, "Fucking loser," under his breath.

"What did you say?"

"Nothing."

"Don't back-talk me, you bugger." Niresh's father turned to his friends and said in Sinhalese, "Look at the tongue on him. Ever since his balls dropped, he thinks he's a big shot."

The men roared with laughter.

Amrith was appalled by his uncle's crudeness towards his own son.

Niresh, who did not know Sinhalese, said, "Yeah, yeah." He turned and sauntered off.

Amrith followed.

As they left, Amrith heard his uncle telling his friends, in Sinhalese, that Niresh was a stone around his neck. He had wanted to pack him off to camp, but Niresh had begged to come here.

Amrith glanced at his cousin, puzzled. What his uncle said contradicted Niresh's story of wanting to attend football camp with his buddies.

They went down to the beach. Most of the sand had been eaten up by the encroaching monsoon sea, and so they walked in the Goat's-Foot that spread its greenery beyond the sand. They got to a flat boulder that jutted out into the sea and Niresh scrambled over it, leaving Amrith to follow him. The waves threw themselves against the boulder with such force, there was a mist in the air. Niresh sat down as close to the edge as he dared. Amrith settled near him.

"So, if you knew I existed, why didn't you get in touch?" Niresh picked up a stone and flung it at the waves.

Amrith took a piece of coral in his hand and examined it, hoping his cousin would not pursue this. But Niresh had turned to him, waiting for a reply.

"How?" Amrith said, without looking at him.

"But you had to know my address. I'm guessing your aunt or uncle wrote and told my dad that your mum had died and they had adopted you. I mean, my dad seemed to already know this when we met your uncle in Fort."

Amrith put the coral back on the rock.

"Come on, Amrith."

"*Um* . . . I . . . I don't want to talk about it."

His cousin stared at him. "Sure, no problem." Niresh threw another stone out to sea.

A kingfisher circled and dipped, circled and dipped over the stormy monsoon waves. Clouds were gathering on the horizon.

Amrith, glancing at Niresh, saw that a gulf had opened up between them.

~~~~~
~~~~~

Once Amrith had been picked up from the hotel that evening and they were driving home, Uncle Lucky stared out of the window for a while, lost in thought. He turned to Amrith. "Remember the story I told you about my father and his brother? And how, years after my father's death, I went to Jaffna to look at that useless piece of land?"

Amrith nodded.

"Well," Uncle Lucky said, clearing his throat. "The story does not end there. You see, my uncle, like my father, had ruined himself in court cases. He had left his widow with very little money. In small towns, the arrival of any stranger is a source of interest. Before I had even left the railway depot, the stationmaster found out who I was. He told me that my aunt had cataracts in both eyes and desperately needed an operation.

"By the time I arrived at her house, she knew I was coming. A neighbor was posted at the gate and he informed me that my aunt would like to invite me in for a cup of tea. I could guess why she was doing so; she was hoping I would help her out of her poverty." He glanced at Amrith. "But I refused to go in." He sighed. "Later, after I married your Aunty Bundle, she convinced me to make amends. But, by then, the widow had died. For a long time, it plagued me that I did not go in and offer her help. I always wondered how her life had ended, what terrible misery she must have sunk into.

"Then, a few years later, when I started my office and was hiring staff, a young woman from Jaffna came to be interviewed. She was from the same village as my father. I felt a curious excitement take hold of me when I found this out. I told her who my father was and she did not recognize his name, but when I mentioned my uncle's name, she was very surprised. It turned out that she was related to my aunt, the widow. Her young niece." He looked at Amrith significantly. He was speaking of Miss Rani. "I not only hired her, but also paid for her to take courses to improve herself and help me run the office. And, you know, the funny thing is, from the moment Miss Rani came to work for me, my business really took off. By accepting my past and making amends, I had become a better businessman. I was more clearheaded and able to see around problems, to spot trickery."

He took his glasses off and wiped them with his hand-kerchief. "Yes-yes, the past is really helpful, if we can come to accept it." He put his glasses back on and regarded Amrith. "And sometimes the past does offer us a gift – a way to come to terms with what has happened to us."

Amrith knew what Uncle Lucky meant by "a gift." His cousin, Niresh.

Rain had started to pock the car windows. Amrith gazed out at the grayness, feeling depressed. The gulf that had come between him and Niresh had stayed for the rest of his visit.

〰〰
〰〰

That evening, Aunt Wilhelmina dropped in for dinner. Her face was shining with triumph. She had barely seated herself before she declared, "Yes, I was right all along. Mervin's return is connected to money." She narrowed her eyes in anger. "Do you know what that blackguard is planning to do? Sell Sanasuma."

Amrith became very still. Sanasuma was the holiday home that had meant so much to his mother. In that time when Aunty Bundle had visited them at the estate, they actually made a trip to see it. He lowered his fork and pressed his hands together under the table.

"Do you remember it, Bundle?" Aunt Wilhelmina continued, unaware of his distress, "You and Asha spent many vacations there."

Aunty Bundle did not reply. She was watching Amrith closely.

Aunt Wilhelmina became aware of his discomfort. "Oh, dear, I'm so sorry, child."

Amrith pushed back his chair. "*Um* . . . could I be excused?"

"Yes, son." Uncle Lucky looked at him, concerned.

As Amrith left the living room, he heard Aunt Wilhelmina say, "Bundle, something must be done. Sanasuma should be Amrith's."

"But what can we do, Aunt Wilhelmina? You know the old man left everything to Mervin in his will."

"It is not right." Aunt Wilhelmina's voice had risen to a birdlike trill. "It was Asha who loved Sanasuma. It meant nothing to Mervin. Amrith should not be robbed of his inheritance. Sanasuma belongs to him."

When Amrith reached his room, he lay on his bed, curled up on his side. *Sana-suma.* As he spoke the word in his mind, the memory of that visit swept over him.

Even though the holiday home was just an hour from their tea estate, his mother had never been able to take him there because she had no car. Aunty Bundle's visit had allowed them to make the trip.

The road to Sanasuma had not been mended in a long time and it was full of potholes. Finally their car could go no further and Amrith, Aunty Bundle, and his mother had walked the last stretch. There had been a smell in the air of eucalyptus, pine, and the dried ancient mud of the path. Amrith had picked off a eucalyptus leaf and pressed its cool sting to his nose. The jungle was all around and the trees closed in, towering above. Through their leaves, the sunlight laid a shifting filigree on the path. Everything was still down there, but they could hear the wind roaring through the treetops. It felt to Amrith as if they were underwater, at the bottom of a river that thundered high above. Occasionally, there was a sound, as if a branch was about to break, and they looked up to see monkeys jumping from tree to tree, swinging down the branches.

Then, in the distance, he heard the chatter of water. The light began to increase ahead. The forest soon fell away to bushes and patches of grass, with brilliant magenta flowers on waving stalks. The underbrush was noisy with the trilling of cicadas, a bird that made a low, mournful *hoop-hoop-hoop.*

The road finally came to an end at a clearing.

The old family home was perched on a shelf of land that jutted out from a mountainside. Above them, around them, were towering mountains, their peaks lost in the clouds. From the shelf, there was a precipitous descent to a densely wooded gorge miles below, flashes of silver from a river that ran through it. The rocky slope of the mountain came down to the back garden of the bungalow and, a little way up the slope, a stream tinkled as it skipped downwards. At one point, there was a drop and the stream tumbled over in a waterfall, then loitered in a rock pool before continuing its journey past the bungalow and over the shelf of land to join the river far below. The sun embroidered sequins into the falling water; the rock pool shimmered like green silk.

As his mother and Aunty Bundle approached the little bungalow, Amrith hurried to keep up with them. It was made completely of wood and was in a terrible state. The pillars of the front veranda had lost most of their paint and the floorboards were broken in places. His mother and Aunty Bundle had to struggle with the door before they got it open.

The moment they entered, they heard the scurry of some animal among the furniture. For fear it might be a snake, they did not go in any further. There were giant cobwebs everywhere and the floor was littered with leaves that had blown in through a shattered windowpane. The upholstery of the sofa and armchairs had great patches of mildew growing on it. As Aunty Bundle and his mother looked around, their faces were sad and angry. Finally, his mother sighed. "Let's leave. We should not have come back."

And yet, once they were walking away from the house, his mother changed her mind. She wanted them to go swimming in the rock pool, as they had planned. They were wearing their bathing suits under their clothes and they stripped down. His mother was the first to go in. She shivered at the coldness, then cried out, "Come, Amrith, come, this is heaven!"

Aunty Bundle lowered Amrith into the water and his mother took him. He gasped from the cold and kicked out frantically, fastening his arms around her neck, his legs around her waist.

"Now relax, Amrith, relax." She drifted away on her back, loosening Amrith's legs, which trailed up in the water. "Are you okay?"

He nodded and clung to her. His mother's arms were strong around him. They warmed his back, his hips. "Amrith," she whispered in his ear, "when you think of this place, I want you to remember what fun we had swimming together."

Before they left that day, his mother took Amrith to the back garden and showed him a eucalyptus tree. On its trunk was carved *Asha and Bundle, Best Friends*.

# IO

# Aunty Bundle Accepts
# the "Gift"

~~~~~~~

The next morning, Amrith found it impossible to concentrate on his typing exercises. He kept glancing towards the door every few minutes, losing his place, and having to start the line over again. Niresh had said he would try and visit today, but Amrith wondered if he would, given the way they had parted yesterday. He watched the time pass on the wall-clock. By eleven, he had given up hope. Miss Rani, whom he found himself looking at differently now, came by to mark his exercises. She circled numerous errors with her red pencil, but he did not care.

Amrith started a new exercise. He had just finished the first line, when the door opened and Niresh rushed in. He was panting from having run up the stairs and his hair was disheveled. He waved as he came across the office.

"What happens when you cross a centipede and a parrot?"

"I don't know." Amrith stood up, grinning.

"You get a walkie-talkie." Niresh snorted. Everyone in the office turned and stared.

He thumped Amrith on the back. Everything had returned to normal between them. "Hey, my dad's got some errands to do. Do you want to hang out for a bit, maybe have some lunch?"

Amrith went to ask Uncle Lucky. He gave his permission, then took out his wallet and handed Amrith a hundred-rupee note. "Go to Pagoda for lunch. But don't let that boy pay. You have enjoyed their hospitality and we need to return it, as best as we can." He looked at Amrith from under his hooded eyelids.

They could not invite Niresh to their home because of Aunty Bundle's refusal to meet these Canadian relatives.

A giddy exhilaration took hold of Amrith and Niresh as they left the office. They ran down the stairs, charging through office workers, and burst out onto Chatham Street.

"Hey," Niresh cried, "I want to buy a sarong."

"Sure," Amrith cried back, in high spirits. "I know where to go."

Amrith took Niresh to Laksala, the government hand-icraft store. It was in an old colonial building with lofty ceilings. As they entered, Amrith pointed to a part of the store that had knickknacks. "Do you want to get gifts for your three friends?"

Niresh looked at him blankly.

"Your three close buddies," Amrith prompted.

"Oh . . . oh, yeah." Niresh glanced away. "No, it's okay."

Amrith led the way to the section that sold clothes. A woman in a Kandyan sari was standing behind a glass counter. When they asked to look at sarongs, she laid out a selection on the counter.

They stood shoulder to shoulder, looking at the sarongs, passing them to each other. Niresh finally picked a green one, with a pattern of dancing peacocks around the border. He wanted to try it on and the woman led them to a curtained dressing room at the back.

Standing outside the dressing room, Amrith could hear Niresh unzipping his shorts, the shuffle of his sandals as he pushed them off to slip into the sarong. He heard the rustle of the sarong being pulled up. There was a moment of stillness and then Niresh said, "Damn . . . Amrith?"

"Yes?"

Niresh pulled open the curtain. He had tied the sarong all gathered and knotted in a way that made the front a good deal shorter than the back. Amrith smiled.

"I look like a freak, don't I?"

"No, it's not too bad."

Amrith indicated with his hands how Niresh should tie the sarong; how he needed to move his hips from side to side before quickly bringing the two ends of the sarong together, then tie a knot and make a roll around his waist.

Niresh tried again, but his effort was a failure. They looked at his handiwork in the mirror. Their eyes met and they laughed.

Niresh turned to him and lifted his arms away from his body. "Okay, I give up. Show me how it's done." He wanted him to step right up, face to face.

Amrith did not look at Niresh as he stood in front of him. His hands were shaking ever so slightly as he began to untie the mess his cousin had made. When he moved the sarong from side to side, before bringing the ends together, he got a glimpse of Niresh's white underpants, the swirl of dark hairs above the waistband.

Once Amrith was done, Niresh looked in the mirror at the neatly tied sarong. "Wow!"

Amrith, too, looked at his cousin in the mirror. When he had stood close to him, there had been a nice smell to Niresh, of well-matured leather.

Amrith took Niresh to Pagoda for lunch. The restaurant was famous in Colombo. The wizened waiters, in their white sarongs and white coats with epaulets and brass buttons, were an institution themselves. For as long as the Manuel-Pillais had been coming here, they were always served by the same waiter – a plump man with a white walrus mustache named Albert. They were his clients and no other waiter dared serve them. The moment they would enter, Albert would come hurrying towards them, waving the white cloth he carried over his arms, crying, "Sir,

Madam, this way." A table would always be found for them. They never waited.

When Amrith and Niresh came into the restaurant, however, Albert sailed right past them to another client, who had actually come in after them. Amrith was mortified. He had hoped to impress his cousin by the way Albert would heartily greet him and deferentially wave them to a table. But the waiter did not even recognize him. Finally, after many more people had been taken ahead of them, a junior waiter led them to a small table at the back in a dark corner. He gave them a suspicious glare as they sat down. Young boys did not dine alone; they did not have the money to do so. He plonked two menus on the table and left.

"What's up?" Niresh asked.

"Nothing."

Yet, Niresh had caught on to the waiter's hostility. He grimaced in commiseration. "Let's just have a good time."

Amrith and the girls usually ordered a selection of cakes and short eats, which were brought to them on tiered serving plates. They would eat what they wanted and then the waiter, who knew just how many items there had been on the plates, would add up the bill. Amrith suggested that they do the same thing now.

After the waiter had grudgingly slammed down the plates and left, Niresh squinted at the assortment before them. "So they count how many are left and add up the bill that way?"

Amrith nodded.

Niresh grinned wickedly. "I see." He pointed to a breaded capsicum stuffed with fish. "Are you going to eat that one?"

Amrith shook his head.

"No, me neither." Niresh picked up the capsicum and winked at Amrith. He gave it a long lick before putting it back on the plate.

Amrith was shocked, but then he grinned. He pointed to an egg cutlet. "Do you want this one?"

Niresh shook his head.

Amrith licked it.

They snorted and giggled. Each of them took the short-eats and cakes they wanted and licked every other one, careful not to leave the trail of their tongues on the icing of cakes.

When the waiter came by to add up the bill, Amrith and Niresh took one look at his sour expression and snuffled with laughter. The waiter glared at them, ripped off the bill, and slammed it down on the table. Usually one paid up at the cash register, but the waiter, knowing something was up, stood by with his arms folded.

Niresh and Amrith reached for the bill at the same time.

"No, Niresh, I have to pay."

Niresh pulled at the bill. "Don't be an ass, Amrith. I asked you out."

"No, I . . . I have to pay. Uncle Lucky will be very upset if I don't."

The seriousness of Amrith's tone made Niresh relinquish the bill.

When they were out on the street, Niresh touched Amrith's arm. "Thanks." Yet, there was a frown on his face.

They walked a short distance, then Niresh came to a stop in the shade of a shop awning. He had adopted the Sri Lankan habit of carrying a handkerchief, and he took it out and mopped his brow and neck. "So," he said, turning to Amrith, "why would your uncle be *upset* if I paid?"

Amrith did not reply. It had slipped out involuntarily.

Niresh was waiting.

Amrith looked at his feet. "It's . . . just a way of returning hospitality, for lunch at Mount Lavinia."

"But why would he be *upset*?" Niresh squeezed his arm. "Come on, Amrith, I'm your cousin. You can tell me."

"No, Niresh, no. It's . . . it's just complicated."

"How?"

Amrith was silent, but then seeing that his cousin would not give up, he said, "It's . . . my aunt. She . . . she doesn't want to have anything to do with you all. She's got many feelings about . . . what happened."

"What did happen, Amrith?"

He did not say anything.

Niresh regarded him, his head to one side. "You know, it's my history, too. Your mum was my aunt. Your grandparents were mine as well. I would like to know why my father disowned you. I get the feeling that he hated your mum. But why?"

"I really don't want to talk about it."

"Why not?"

"Because I don't." Amrith rounded on his cousin. "Why can't you respect that and leave me alone?" He stalked away and, after a moment, Niresh followed a few steps behind.

Before they parted company in front of Uncle Lucky's office building, Niresh touched his shoulder and said, with a tentative smile, "I'll see you around?"

"Of course." Amrith forced himself to smile.

His cousin began to walk away.

"Hey, Niresh."

"Yeah?" He turned.

"How about a parting joke?"

Niresh grinned. "Okay, you asked for it. What do you get when you cross a stripper with a banana?"

Amrith had heard this before, but he dutifully replied, "I don't know."

"A self-peeling banana!"

Everything appeared restored between them.

~~~~~

Since their first meeting with Niresh and his father two days ago, Uncle Lucky had been troubled by Aunty Bundle's stand on Amrith's relatives. That evening, while Amrith was up on the terrace feeding the birds, he heard them arguing in the side garden, their voices drifting up to him.

"No, Lucky, no, I will not have anything to do with them. Especially now, with Mervin robbing Amrith of Sanasuma. Stop asking me all the time. My first loyalty is to the memory of Asha."

"And what about our boy, Bundle, what is your loyalty to him? Mervin and Niresh are, after all, his family."

"Lucky! We are his family."

"But, Bundle, they are his blood relatives. And the boys are getting along so well. Surely you have noticed the change in Amrith."

Aunty Bundle was silent.

"You have to invite Niresh to our house."

"*Ah,* Lucky, don't ask me to do that."

"This is Amrith's home. You say we are his family, but by forcing our boy to meet his cousin in Fort or at Mount Lavinia, you're actually making him feel a stranger here."

Aunty Bundle was silent for a long while. "I . . . I need some time to think about this."

Amrith was lying down the next afternoon when Aunty Bundle knocked on his door and came into the room.

"Son," she said, standing by his bed, "I've called your cousin and invited him to spend the day. Tomorrow, after I'm driven to work, Mendis will go by the hotel and pick him up." She tried to smile, but failed. For a while she was silent, her fingers drumming on the bedpost as she looked past the French windows into the side garden.

"Amrith, when I get back from work this evening, we must go to the Mount Lavinia Hotel. Since I have invited your cousin, good form requires that I must pay your uncle a courtesy visit."

〰〰〰〰

When their car pulled up in front of the hotel that evening, Niresh was waiting for them by the front steps.

Amrith was the first to get out. His cousin hurried forward and shook his hand without a word. He did not smile and glanced anxiously at Aunty Bundle, who was still in the car. Dreading this encounter, she was taking her time, telling Mendis about an errand she needed run.

Once the car had left, Aunty Bundle stood for a moment in the driveway, not looking at Niresh. She straightened the neckline of her blouse and pushed her handbag up under her arm. Then, with a deep breath, she came towards them.

"Hello, dear, how are you?" She smiled, but did not look him in the eye as they shook hands. "I am very pleased to finally meet you. I'm sorry I have not had you over before, but what with my work and everything, I haven't had a moment. Now come-come, Amrith, let's go and see your uncle."

And with that, she hurried ahead of them into the foyer.

His uncle was expecting them on the terrace and Aunty Bundle led the way up there. Niresh and Amrith followed in silence.

When Aunty Bundle saw his uncle across the terrace, she was still for a moment, a great sadness passing over her face. She struggled to compose herself, then walked across to him, her head held high.

His uncle rose slowly from his seat, straightening his shirt, flattening his hair.

When Aunty Bundle reached the table, they both stood staring at each other.

"Hello, Mervin."

"Hello, Bundle."

In the pool, some children were calling to each other in a foreign language. There was a tinkling of glasses and ice from the bar.

"Thank you for inviting Niresh to spend the day," his uncle said. "It is very nice of you." There was a sheepish expression on his face.

"It's a pleasure. The boys seem to be getting on so well, it would be nice for Amrith to have his cousin come home."

She smiled at Niresh and Amrith. "Now, why don't you boys walk around a bit and leave us adults to catch up?"

They left them alone but, without a word being spoken between the cousins, they did not go too far, as if fearing something bad might happen in their absence. They stayed at the other end of the terrace, making feeble attempts at conversation, but all the while looking in the direction of the adults.

His uncle and Aunty Bundle did not appear to be saying very much. They sat in awkward silence, every so often exchanging a few words. After a while, Aunty Bundle got up and shook his uncle's hand. She came across the terrace and, as she drew near, Amrith could see how tense she was.

When they were in the car, Aunty Bundle leaned back against the seat and closed her eyes. A sweat had broken out on her forehead and she scrambled through her handbag, took out her handkerchief, and mopped her face. Her hand was shaking.

Aunty Bundle dropped Amrith at the gates of their house, saying there was one more errand she had to run.

When she came home, an hour later, the rest of the family were out in the courtyard. Her sarong was dirty from kneeling in soil; she had been to his mother's grave. Yet, instead of returning with red eyes, as she usually did, she was almost smiling. This meeting with his uncle had been difficult, but it seemed to have brought her some reconciliation with the past.

Uncle Lucky was seated in a Planter's chair having a drink and, attracted by the radiance of her face, he took hold of her hand as she went by.

Aunty Bundle laughed as if she were a girl, and pulled her hand away. "What is this, men, embarrassing me." She passed on into the house.

Amrith looked after her and felt a grudging respect.

# I I

# Kassanava

~~~~~~~

The next morning, Amrith had dressed and eaten his breakfast before anyone else. After Mendis went to pick up Niresh, he wandered around the courtyard, then went to his room, only to come out again.

Selvi passed by and caught him dawdling under the jak tree. "Waiting for your boyfriend?"

He gave her a disdainful glare.

She giggled and went on her way.

Mendis finally returned with his cousin. Amrith rushed forward to greet Niresh as he stepped out of the car. They grinned at each other and shook hands warmly, Amrith trying not to flinch at his cousin's grip.

Eva, Zsa Zsa, and Magda had come running out of the living room, wagging their tails. They crowded around the stranger.

"Just ignore them, Niresh. *Shoo!* They're a real nuisance."

But his cousin had got down on one knee and was saying in a high silly voice, "Well, hello, girl. Yes, hello to you too and you too."

The dogs were beside themselves. They rolled over on their backs, stuck their legs in the air, and made pedaling gestures, their tongues lolling out foolishly as Niresh scratched their stomachs.

Aunty Bundle was approaching and Niresh stood up.

"Hello, dear, welcome-welcome." Her smile was genuine, unlike the last time they met. She shook his hand and then, seeing that Niresh was hot and sweaty, she said to Amrith, "Haven't you offered your cousin a glass of thambili, yet? *Ttttch,* how inhospitable. Haven't I taught you children anything? The boy is not used to our climate, *nah.*" She beamed up at Niresh. "Have you had thambili before?"

"No, ma'am, I haven't," Niresh said, his voice and demeanor deferential.

"It's coconut water. Very good for quenching thirst. Now, do you eat crabs, dear?"

"Yes, ma'am, I do."

"Good-good. I'll send my Mendis to the market for crabs. There's a new moon, which is the perfect time to get them. They don't scurry about, as they would under a full moon, and so will be nice and succulent."

"Thank you, ma'am. That would very nice."

She smiled up at him again. "You must call me Aunty, dear. In Sri Lanka, that's how we address older people." She

touched his arm. "Now you must treat our home as yours."
She bustled back into the house, calling, "Jane-Nona!
Jane-Nona! I need the shopping list." The dogs followed
after her.

His cousin was charmed by Aunty Bundle.

"Mala, Mala, hurry, men, we're going to be late." Selvi
sauntered into the living room, looking back, calling to her
sister. She was pretending not to have seen Niresh.

Niresh became a little uneasy. Amrith had assured him
that the girls had forgiven him for teasing them, although
they really hadn't.

"I'm coming, men," Mala yelled, also for effect, and
hurried across the living room with her cloth bag over one
shoulder.

They came out into the courtyard and stopped, pretending to be surprised to see Niresh. Their charade irritated
Amrith.

"Mala, Selvi," he said, "this is Niresh."

"Oh, hello." They nodded at him coolly, standing at a
distance.

"It's great to meet you guys." Niresh went towards
them, with his most charming smile, and offered his hand.

They shook it after a brief hesitation.

"Listen, I'm sorry for what I said on the phone the
other day."

"We didn't care." Selvi glared at him.

"Yeah," Niresh said, smiling, "I know, you guys are
good sports. But, anyway, I felt I should apologize."

"We have a nickname for you," Selvi declared.

"Akka, don't." Mala suppressed a smile.

"Oh, yeah?" Niresh grinned, knowing this was his punishment. "What?"

"Kassanava. It's Sri Lankan for 'Casanova'."

The girls giggled and even Amrith couldn't help smiling. "Kassanava" meant "an irritating itch."

Niresh grinned gamely and bowed to concede that he accepted this nickname as penance. And now the air was cleared between them.

"So, I hear you're both big fans of Shaun Cassidy," Niresh said. "I think he's amazing, too."

"You do?" Selvi hugged her books to her chest, thrilled to meet a fellow devotee.

"Yeah, sure." Niresh nodded with great enthusiasm, his hair bouncing up and down.

Amrith was, as always, astonished at how smoothly his cousin lied. He had made a gagging noise when Amrith mentioned Shaun Cassidy.

"He's super popular in Canada," Niresh continued. "I've met Shaun in person." His chest expanded. "He was signing records at this store downtown and I went and lined up and got my record autographed."

"You met him in person?" the girls cried.

"Yeah, sure. I stood with him and had my photo taken. He's such a cool guy. He even put his arm around my shoulder when they were taking the photo."

Selvi and Mala were in awe. The possibility of them ever meeting Shaun Cassidy was nonexistent. And here Niresh had actually been touched by the star.

"Have you seen *The Hardy Boys Mysteries* on TV?" Niresh asked.

"You have seen *Hardy Boys!*" Selvi sighed.

"We're dying to see it," Mala added, "but we'll never get it here until we're probably twenty."

"It was great. Everyone in Canada was watching it. Do you know Shaun Cassidy's going to be in a new series, this fall?"

"Really?"

"Yeah, it's called *Breaking Away.*" He began to tell Selvi and Mala whatever little he knew about it. They listened, eating up every word.

Amrith was beginning to feel annoyed at the way his sisters were monopolizing Niresh and he was glad to see Aunty Bundle come out into the courtyard.

"Girls, girls," she called to them, "let's get along."

Selvi and Mala followed their mother reluctantly.

The moment their backs were turned, Niresh winked at Amrith.

He grinned back, feeling his resentment disappear. "Selvi's probably going to tell her friends about you the moment she gets to tuition," he said in an undertone, as they smiled and waved to the girls while the car reversed onto the road.

"Are her friends good-looking?" Niresh asked.

"*Yuk,* no."

"Real dogs, *eh?*"

"Yeah, real dogs."

Once the car left, Amrith led Niresh into the house to get him a drink. As they went across the living room, he told his cousin how he referred to Selvi's friends as the SNOTs.

Niresh roared and gave Amrith a mighty clap on his back to show his approval.

In the pantry, as Amrith poured out a glass of thambili, Niresh asked, his head to one side, "So your sisters really don't have boyfriends?"

Amrith shook his head.

Niresh frowned as he pondered this. Amrith could not tell if his cousin agreed or not with the rule.

After they had finished their drinks, Amrith gave Niresh a tour of the house, trailed by Eva, Zsa Zsa, and Magda.

Their house had, of course, been built by Lucien Lindamulagé. He often brought architecture students over to show them the house. Amrith had heard the architect's tour often and knew the features of the house well. As he took his cousin around, he pointed out how the house was modeled on precolonial homes – that unlike Western architecture, the rooms opened into each other and out to the gardens and courtyard, to allow for the maximum flow of air, thus keeping the house cool; the way one could stand anywhere and there would be a sense of vistas opening up all around, the darkness of interiors contrasting with the brightness of exteriors; the way Amrith's room was entered from a door in what seemed the boundary wall but, instead, led to new quarters – a representation of the women's quarters, the zenana, with its secluded walled garden. He showed Niresh the century-old doors and windows that Lucien Lindamulagé had scoured the country to find. Amrith pointed out how, above each window, there was a rectangle of intricately carved wood latticework, known as a mal lallie, which let in cool air even when the window was closed.

He led Niresh up to the terrace and his cousin's eyes grew wide at the sight of the aviary. When Amrith told him it was his birthday gift, Niresh shook his head and said, with a laugh, "Man, you're spoilt." He took Niresh inside so he could feed Kuveni a piece of mango.

~~~~~
~~~~~

Jane-Nona made her famous crab curry in honor of Niresh's visit, with her own combination of roasted spices ground into a paste, coconut milk, murunga leaves, and tamarind to give it a nice tang. Aunty Bundle and Uncle Lucky showed Niresh how to eat the crabs using his teeth to break the softer parts of the shell, how to suck out the flesh from the legs.

For a while they were silent, enjoying the crabs, then the girls began to ply Niresh with questions about Canada. Had he eaten at McDonald's and Kentucky Fried Chicken? Did the burgers and fries and milkshakes and chicken and coleslaw taste as extraordinarily delicious as they had heard and read? They had not received replies to the questions they had sent through Amrith, and so they asked Niresh if he had seen *A Little Romance*. Did he go to a school that had both boys and girls in it? Did people have their own personal lockers in his school? Go to proms? Drive cars? Go on dates to movies?

Amrith could tell his cousin was surprised by their fascination with mundane things. Yet, he gamely answered their questions with great seriousness and, after a while, Amrith got the distinct feeling that his cousin had begun to exaggerate the glamor of Canada. He wondered, for the first time, if everything his cousin said about Canada was true.

Niresh was on his best behavior with Aunty Bundle and Uncle Lucky, but he relaxed enough to start calling them Aunty and Uncle.

While they were having dessert, Selvi asked Niresh if he would like to come to the club that afternoon for a swim. His cousin was keen and so Amrith had to agree, even though he did not want to go. Selvi's friends were probably going to be there. Niresh would be even more monopolized.

Mala was not joining them as she had to visit the tailor and be measured for her party dress.

On the way to the club, Selvi taught Niresh how to say, "hello, how are you," in Sinhalese. *Mama loku gembek.* She wanted him to greet her friends this way.

What she was really teaching him was, "I am a big frog."

Amrith was beginning to read his cousin – when his eyes were particularly wide with innocence, he was usually lying or leading someone on. Niresh knew he was not learning a Sinhalese greeting. Yet, he attempted the phrase over and over again, with great sincerity, as if keen to get it right.

He treated Selvi to a joke – "What do you get when you cross an ostrich with a Big Mac? A bird that buries its head in a sandwich." He roared at his own wit, not noticing that Selvi looked at him a little askance.

~~~~
~~~~

The Lord Louis Mountbatten Club was a white-stuccoed building with a pillared portico and magenta bougainvilleas climbing up its walls. It had been White Only until about twenty years ago. Even after Independence, it had remained restricted for a while, and any white sailor in town, no matter how low his rank, could get a locker at the club, while even the prime minister was not allowed to enter. Now, most of its members were Sri Lankan.

Once the car had dropped them off, Amrith signed his cousin in and led Niresh through the building, with its high ceilings and arches. A series of French windows opened out onto a terrace, with rattan chairs and wrought iron tables on it. His cousin seemed impressed by the club with its liveried waiters who rushed back and forth.

Selvi was hurrying ahead of them, down the steps that led to the garden and the swimming pool. The SNOTs, on seeing Selvi, leapt up from their lounging chairs and looked eagerly past her for the cousin from abroad.

"Let's go check out the babes." Niresh grinned at Amrith.

Amrith smiled thinly. All through lunch and in the car ride here, he had barely had a chance to say a word to Niresh.

As they walked through the garden, Selvi's friends adjusted their clothing nervously. They had taken extra trouble with their hair, and even wore a bit of makeup.

"Now, Niresh," Selvi commanded, "say hello to my friends in Sinhalese."

With sincere goodwill, he offered his hand to one of them. "Mama loku gembek."

The girls shrieked so loudly that people on the terrace turned to look at them. They began to laugh, holding on to each other, saying "mama loku gembek," over and over again, all the time giving Niresh little covert glances. It was clear they found him, if not handsome, at least glamorous for being from abroad.

Niresh winked at Amrith. The joke was on the girls.

Niresh and Amrith already had their swimsuits on and they went to the men's room to take off their clothes and hang them up.

When they came back to the pool, the girls were still changing. Niresh gestured towards a pillar not far from the pool. They hid behind it and grinned at each other.

Selvi and her friends came out in their bathing suits. They stood at the edge of the pool. Niresh gave Amrith a signal and, yelling at the top of their lungs, they rushed at the girls, who spun around shrieking. They cried out as they were pushed in, then wailed, coughed up water, and berated the boys. Amrith and Niresh leapt in after them, making them shriek all over again.

Soon a water fight was in progress, Amrith and Niresh trying to swim underwater and grab their legs, the girls kicking out and splashing them as they tried to escape. All of them were reveling in a game they knew they were too old to be playing.

They got raucous and Nandasena and Mrs. Kuruvilla, the attendants at the men's and women's change rooms, came down to tell them to be quiet or they would complain to their parents. The generosity of their tips and New Year gifts depended on their making sure decorum was main-tained when the parents were absent.

Niresh broke away from the girls. He signaled to Amrith and they swam to the deep end. They clung to the side rail. Niresh shook the hair out of his eyes. "Man, I really need a smoke."

He and Amrith went off to the change room. They wiped down their bodies, grabbed their T-shirts, and Niresh put a packet of cigarettes into his pocket.

There was a shed in one corner, where the pool cleaning equipment was kept. They slipped into the narrow space between it and the parapet wall. Niresh lit a cigarette, drew on it hungrily, and breathed out a long stuttering breath.

*"Boo!"* Selvi and her friends stood staring at them.

"Shit." Niresh hid his cigarette behind his back.

"Give us a puff," Selvi said, holding out her hand.

"No way."

"Yes way. Otherwise I'm telling my parents you made Amrith smoke."

After a moment, Niresh grinned, knowing he was defeated. He held the cigarette out. Selvi drew on it and immediately began to cough, bending over and clutching her chest.

"You girls and boys, what are you doing here?" They spun around to find Mrs. Kuruvilla standing with her hands on her hips.

Selvi and the SNOTs turned and fled, followed by Mrs. Kuruvilla. Niresh signaled to Amrith and they leapt over the short boundary wall. They hurried away, laughing and shaking their heads.

They walked along the railway line, while Niresh finished his cigarette. Amrith was glad to have his cousin to himself.

Niresh put his arm around his shoulder. "So, are you a tits-man or an arse-man?"

Amrith thought desperately – tits, arse, tits, arse – this could be important, like which sports team you supported. "*Um,* arse."

"Yeah! Alright! Me, too." Niresh gave him a mighty whack on the shoulders.

Despite the sting spreading through his shoulders, Amrith felt a great relief to have given the right answer.

They sat on some rocks that bordered the beach. The shore below had been eaten up by the monsoon waves, which came right up to the boulders. Niresh took a last drag of his cigarette and threw the butt into the sea. His face became grave. "So, I have bad news. Tomorrow, I'm going with my dad to stay, for a few weeks, at some place outside Colombo. He says he has some business to do there."

His uncle was going to try and sell Sanasuma. Yet Amrith, at the moment, did not care about this. "*Ah,* do you have to go?"

"Yeah." His cousin frowned, gazing out at the sea, his face gloomy. "What else would I do?"

"Niresh . . . perhaps . . . perhaps you could come and stay with us!"

"You think?"

"Would you like to?"

"Yeah, of course. That'd be great."

"I'm sure Uncle Lucky and Aunty Bundle will say yes."

Niresh laughed and clapped Amrith on the back, nearly knocking him off the rock. "And here I thought I was going to have to leave, just when we were getting to be friends, you know what I mean?"

Amrith nodded. He did know.

Amrith was certain Uncle Lucky and Aunty Bundle would agree to Niresh staying with them, as they maintained an easy hospitality at their house. He was more worried about Niresh's father. Though Amrith felt sure that his uncle would be glad to leave Niresh behind, he wondered if he might refuse to let his son stay with the Manuel-Pillais, out of spite.

When they got back from the club, he went looking for Aunty Bundle. Her face became very serious as he made his request. "You know, son, that *I* would love to have your cousin to stay, but your uncle . . ." She sighed. "Let's you and I take Niresh back this evening."

He saw that she, too, suspected his uncle might refuse, just to be nasty.

When they entered the Mount Lavinia Hotel, Niresh led the way up the stairs and along the corridor towards the terrace. Amrith could tell that he was worried about what state his father would be in. As they approached the terrace, they could hear the mirthless crack of his uncle's laugh, the guffaws of the other men.

Aunty Bundle came to a stop when she saw his uncle. Her face turned to stone. He sat with his legs sprawled out, the empty bottle of arrack before him. The men with him were thuggish-looking and peppered their English with vulgar Sinhalese idioms, referring to each other as "oo" and "oomba," using derogatory verbs like "vareng" and "palayang." Aunty Bundle would not approach men who were in such a state of intoxication. She sent Niresh to fetch his father.

"*Ah*, you bloody bugger, returned, have you?" his uncle cried, as Niresh came up to him.

Niresh leaned close to his father and spoke to him softly.

His uncle peered in their direction. He tried to rise out of his chair, nearly did not make it, but finally tottered to his feet. He straightened his shirt, flattened his hair, and came towards them. He stopped a little distance away, regarding them with hostility.

"Hello, Mervin."

"Yes, Bundle, what can I do for you?" Alcohol had removed the thin veneer of civility that his uncle had been able to maintain on their last visit.

Niresh was looking anxiously at his father.

"I understand, Mervin, that you are going to be traveling outstation for a while," Aunty Bundle said.

He nodded, but looked guarded. Amrith could tell that he was wondering if they knew about Sanasuma.

"The boys, well, they've been getting on like a house on fire and they seem keen to continue seeing each other and so –"

"Dad," Niresh broke in, "can I stay with Amrith while you're away? Please."

His uncle's expression was unreadable.

"The boys seem really keen, Mervin, they really do," Aunty Bundle said.

They all looked at him, beseechingly.

His uncle's chest expanded; he stood up straighter. "Niresh, I expect you to come with me and I am very angry that you would rather pass time with strangers than with your own father."

Niresh's face flushed.

"You are coming with me, and that is that." His uncle gave them the briefest nod, then walked away.

They went back through the hotel in silence. When they were at the front doors, Aunty Bundle touched Amrith's arm. "Son, I'll give you a few minutes to say good-bye."

Amrith saw what she meant. It was good-bye forever. His uncle, out of spitefulness, was unlikely to permit them to meet again.

The moment Aunty Bundle was gone, Niresh grabbed his arm tightly. "I'm not done with that jerk, I'm not."

Amrith's eyes filled with tears. He did not believe Niresh could make his father change his mind.

"Don't worry, Amrith, I'll fix things, I will."

A tear ran down Amrith's cheek.

"Hey, buddy." Niresh hugged him tight. "I can make my dad change his mind, I can," he whispered in his ear.

Amrith broke away and ran through the hotel doors.

~~~~~~

As they drove home, it began to rain. Aunty Bundle looked out of the car window, a melancholy expression on her face. As for Amrith, he knew now what he felt towards his uncle. Hatred.

It was still raining when they got home and, as Amrith and Aunty Bundle hurried inside, they heard the phone ringing. They entered the living room just as Jane-Nona was picking up the receiver. She turned to them. "Amrith-babba, it's for you."

He rushed to get it.

"See, I told you!" Niresh cried. "I'm coming to stay."

Amrith could not speak for the surge of joy that rose in him. "You are?" he finally blurted. "Are you sure?"

"Yeah, sure I'm sure. So, what do you have to say?"

"I . . . I'm so happy."

"Yeah, me too, Amrith, me too." There was a tenderness in his voice that Amrith had not heard before.

Amrith went to tell Aunty Bundle the good news. She was helping Jane-Nona move a tin tub under the hole in the roof, the barrel having already filled up with rain. She paused in the middle of her task to express her delight.

Afterwards, he longed to be by himself, to savor this wonderful turn of events. Just a few minutes ago, he had been sure he would never see his cousin again and that his life would settle back into its lonely routine, with only typing and the upcoming *Othello* rehearsals offering any relief. Now the future seemed bright again.

When it stopped raining, he went up to the terrace and let himself into the aviary. As he fed his birds, he thought of how, in just five days, such a strong bond had formed between him and Niresh. It felt like he had known his cousin for much longer. Nearly losing Niresh like this had made him realize he loved his cousin. And he knew that his cousin loved him, too.

# 12

# Kinross Beach

~~~~~~
~~~~~~

Later, when the girls found out from Amrith that Niresh was coming to stay, they were overjoyed. Yet, their jubilation made him wary. They had monopolized Niresh for large parts of the day and he did not want that happening during his cousin's stay.

His fears were confirmed that very evening. He was in the aviary, cleaning up and preparing things for the night, when Mala and Selvi came up to the terrace and let themselves into the cage. Their faces were bright with excitement.

"Amrith," Selvi said, as they joined him in the hexagonal flight area, "guess what? I told my friend Tanuja about Niresh coming to stay and she has invited him — and you, too, of course — to spend the day with us girls, at her father's hotel in Bentota. Isn't that wonderful?"

"Yes-yes, Amrith," Mala added, "now Niresh will get to see a little bit of the countryside, *nah*. He was telling us that he has not yet been out of Colombo."

Amrith glanced briefly at the sisters and went back to sweeping the floor.

"So? Don't you think it's a wonderful plan?" Selvi asked, a slight pucker appearing on her forehead.

Amrith stooped down to collect the dirt, then put it into a bin. He took his time, keeping her standing there without an answer. Finally he turned to them. "No, I don't think it's a wonderful plan at all."

"But why, Amrith?" Mala asked, in surprise. "It's such a jolly day trip. And the hotel is famous for its massive pool and delicious lunch buffet and –"

"Look," he said fiercely, "Niresh is my cousin and he is only here for three weeks. I want to spend that time with *just* him. Not with a bunch of stupid girls who are constantly giggling and carrying on and acting like fast-pieces."

Selvi flushed at his calling her and the SNOTs fast-pieces. "Don't be so jealous," she said, looking him up and down with disdain. "You don't own Niresh. And how rude of you. Here Tanuja kindly offers to have your cousin, a stranger, to her hotel and you –"

"Kindness? Rubbish! Tanuja just wants a foreign boyfriend."

"That's not true, she was being nice. She has a very generous nature and is –"

"If she is so generous, why didn't she invite me before Niresh arrived, *ah?* You and your friends had already planned this trip, weeks ago, and you never thought to invite me. Now that I have a foreign cousin, you want me to come. No, I won't, and I won't ask Niresh, either."

He pushed past Selvi and went into the shelter area, where he began to fill up the feeders with seed.

"Fine." Selvi stormed past him on her way out. "You claim to like your cousin, but all you want to do is deny him pleasure. You're selfish. *I'm* going to ask Niresh. Why should he suffer because of your –"

"Don't you dare talk to him about it," Amrith yelled. "If you do, I'll . . . I'll . . ."

"You'll what?" Selvi made a dismissive sound. She put one hand on her hip and wagged her finger. "If I want to ask him, I will. You can't do anything about it."

She let herself out of the safety porch onto the terrace. As a parting shot, she flung at him, "Maybe Niresh will come with us and you can stay at home!"

Amrith went back to filling the feeders, his hands shaking. He felt furious and yet desperate at the same time. Selvi and her friends wanted to draw Niresh into their world, and he had already seen that his cousin was amenable to this. If they monopolized Niresh, Amrith would have to tag along silently, largely ignored. These three weeks were so precious. It was already bad enough that he would have to start attending rehearsals again in eleven days and spend mornings away from Niresh. Now it looked like the girls would be intruding on the time he did have alone with him.

"Amrith." He turned to find Mala regarding him sympathetically. "I'll talk to akka about it." She touched his arm. "You're right. You have only three weeks with your cousin and you should spend all the time you possibly can with him."

Her sympathy made him suddenly teary. He turned away, shrugging her hand off. "It's just not fair," he said, after a moment. "Selvi has so many friends and now she wants to try and take away the one person I have."

"Yes, I know, I know," Mala said soothingly. "I'll have a chat with akka."

By the time they went to bed that night, Mala had talked to her sister. Selvi was no longer angry and, in fact, joked about the whole thing. She presented Amrith with an itinerary she had drawn up for Niresh's three weeks here. Beside each activity, she had written *Amrith not included.*

He knew this was her way of saying sorry, and so he took the joke in good grace.

Amrith wanted to spend every minute he could with Niresh, and the thought of having to practice his typing each morning, in addition to rehearsals, was unbearable. He went to ask Uncle Lucky to let him off.

Uncle Lucky, after some token resistance and a lecture on the hazards of sloth, agreed to free him from typing until his cousin left.

~~~~
~~~~

The next day, when Niresh arrived, the boys stood for a long moment, looking at each other. It seemed to Amrith, as he took his cousin's suitcase from him, that there was a new depth of affection between them.

Niresh had not swum in the sea yet. Because of the monsoon, the waves were too high, the pull of the current dangerous. Amrith suggested that they try Kinross Beach. With the reef not far out, it was relatively safe.

Kinross was only ten minutes away. They went down their street to the railway lines that ran alongside the sea, and walked beside them until they got to their destination.

When they reached Kinross, Amrith saw that the beach was half its usual width and the encroaching sea had pushed the sand up into banks. He signaled to Niresh, and they made their way to a grove of coconut trees. They stripped down to their trunks. The sky was clear, with clouds like lengths of gauze fluttering by. The sea, despite its swell, was a brilliant blue, tipped with emerald green.

When they got to the sea, Amrith went in up to his ankles. The water was cool. He never liked to plunge in and, instead, preferred to wade out slowly, hugging himself. Niresh, however, splashed out and, the moment it was deep enough, he dove into the water with a whoop. He swam out swiftly, then turned around and let a wave carry him back.

"Am-rith, Am-rith," he intoned, as he drifted close to him, "time to go in." Niresh splashed some water at him.

Amrith grinned. "Fuck off."

Niresh pretended to be absolutely shocked. He wagged his finger at him and, in mock-punishment, splashed him again.

Amrith feebly splashed back.

Niresh laughed wickedly and began to circle him. "Time to go under, cousin."

Amrith quickly sank down into the water and came up spluttering. He pushed his hair back and wiped the water off his face.

"There, isn't that better?"

Amrith nodded.

Niresh was looking at him, smiling oddly.

"What?"

His cousin shook his head. "*Nah,* you wouldn't understand."

"Yes, I would. Come on."

"Okay, but don't take this the wrong way."

Amrith drifted closer.

"You and your sisters, even their friends, you guys are all about my age, but you seem much younger." He held up his hands. "It's not a bad thing. I really like it, because I'm having so much fun. But I see that you guys can afford to act young because everything is taken care of in your life. There are always people to watch out for you. I mean, even those damn change-room attendants at the club."

Amrith was silent, absorbing this. He had never thought of his life as being this way.

"So," Niresh said, splashing some water at him, "aren't you going to ask me how I got my dad to change his mind?"

Amrith *had* wondered.

"I told him that I was going to be so bad at school that the authorities would take me away from him and send me to live with my mum."

Amrith wanted to know if he would like to do this, but he did not dare ask.

"I wouldn't go, of course," Niresh said, as if he had read his mind. "I hate her. She's married to this rancher in Alberta and is happy as a pig in shit. I mean, sure she calls me every so often, but that's just her guilty conscience. This one time, I went to visit her in Alberta. Her new husband — he's a Jesus-freak — thought he could act like my father and tell me what to do. He tried to send me to a Christian camp. I told him to go fuck himself. So he hit me. Can you believe it? And she just stood by and didn't do anything. So I went to my room and began to pack and she came in and started trying to make me stay, telling me that he was a good man, and that people in rural Alberta raised their children differently than what I was used to. I guess she must've thought I deserved it, *eh*. I threatened to call the police unless they put me on the next flight back to Toronto."

Niresh's face had grown increasingly angry. He turned and thrashed out into the sea. Amrith knew not to go out to him. As Amrith bobbed up and down in the water, he found himself thinking of how his uncle had wanted to pack Niresh off to camp, but his cousin had begged to come here instead. The more Amrith got to know Niresh, the more he felt that Niresh's life in Canada was not as much fun as he made it out to be. He did not know enough about that country to be able to tell if Niresh's stories – about being on the football team with his three friends and all the things they did together – were true, but he suspected some of them were made up.

When they got back to the house, they used a shower in the side garden that had been built for rinsing off after sea-baths. Amrith found himself watching Niresh, the way he stretched his arms above him and held his head back, the way the water trickled down his stomach. Niresh noticed that Amrith was looking at him. He grinned and splashed some water at him. Amrith grinned back.

In the bedroom, Amrith waited for Niresh to use the bathroom first, as he might want to shower properly with soap and shampoo.

Jane-Nona had taken his cousin's clothes out of the suitcase and put them on shelves in Amrith's almirah and in the chest of drawers. Niresh went through his clothes in the almirah and threw a pair of white underpants, denim shorts, and a red golf shirt onto the bed. "So you've told me that most Sri Lankans don't have vacuum cleaners or dish-washers. But what about washing machines?" He came and stood by the bedpost. "I mean, what do you guys do with dirty clothes?"

"We wash them by hand."

"*You* wash your jeans and shirts by hand?"

"No, there's a woman who comes once a week and washes the clothes."

"Neat."

Niresh pulled his trunks down his thighs and let them fall to the floor. "When we were coming in from the airport, we saw these women beating clothes on rocks." He picked up his towel and pulled it back and forth between his thighs, his penis bouncing up and down. "Does your woman do it that way?"

"Yes." It was not so, but Amrith could not think anymore. The blood was thudding through his head. He had not seen his cousin, nor, in fact, any man naked before.

Niresh swung around. "Am I in your way?"

"*Umm.*"

Actually, he was. Amrith had to get a change of clothes. He went past Niresh to the almirah. There was a mirror on the inside of the door. As Amrith crouched down to search for his clothes, he looked covertly at Niresh's reflection. Sri Lankan men were modest and did not strip down in front of each other.

His cousin was bigger than he was, tight curls clustering around his heavy penis and testicles. Unlike him, Niresh was circumcised, a dark purple ring where the shaft ended, the head curiously vulnerable and exposed. His eyes traveled upwards and he found his cousin looking at him, a slight smile on his face. With a quick movement, Amrith straightened up, grabbed his shirt, his shorts, and his underpants from a shelf. Niresh had begun to pull on his underwear, facing away from Amrith.

"I need . . . I need to use the toilet." Amrith hurried into the bathroom. Once there, he shut the door and leaned against it, his eyes closed. After a moment, he placed his clothes over a rail and pulled down his trunks. His penis sprang up. He looked down at it in dismay.

"Amrith, Amrith." Niresh was calling out from the other side of the bathroom door.

"*Um* . . . what . . . yes?"

"I'm going out to the courtyard, okay?"

"Yes . . . I'll see you there."

The moment the bedroom door closed, Amrith lowered the lid on the toilet, sat down on it, and leaned his head back against the coolness of the cistern. He closed his eyes and tried one of his remedies – reciting "If" by Rudyard Kipling. When that failed he tried the prayer "Hail Holy Queen." Finally he got up and willed himself to urinate, the one thing he was certain would end this embarrassment.

When Amrith came out to the courtyard, Niresh was talking to Mala.

"So you guys never go to concerts?"

She shook her head.

"Back in Canada, we go all the time. Especially in the summer. Who do you like?"

"Anne Murray."

"Seen her. Who else?"

"Olivia Newton-John."

"Ditto."

Mala was impressed.

Niresh had seen Amrith, and he waved to him. As Amrith went across to join his cousin, he tried to stifle a feeling of shame that welled up in him.

The girls had been very good about not monopolizing Niresh, and Mala tried to slip away, making an excuse. Amrith, however, asked her to stay and chat with them. He did not want to be alone with his cousin for once.

~~~~

That night, when they were in bed and had switched off the lights, Niresh lay with his hands behind his head for a while. Then he cleared his throat. "Your mum, she was really pretty."

Amrith turned towards him quickly.

His cousin glanced at him and then away. "I looked in the album. I guess Jane-Nona left it out by mistake, while she was clearing a drawer for me."

Amrith lay on his back and stared at the ceiling. His arms were by his sides, his fists clenched.

"What was she like, Amrith? She seemed like a really fun person in the photographs."

"*Um* . . . I don't remember."

Niresh sat up in bed. "You don't remember her at all?"

"No."

"Shit," his cousin said softly. Then, "What about your father? Do you remember him?"

Amrith held his breath for a long moment, then slowly released it. "No."

"My dad told me that they died in an accident, but he never told me what happened and I was wondering. . . ."

"Niresh."

"Yeah?"

"Please. I . . . I don't want to talk about it. I can't. I just can't. Please."

His cousin looked at him. "Hey, it's okay, Amrith. I understand." He lay down again.

In the distance a train passed by, its whistle long and mournful, its wheels clacking against the tracks. The roar of the sea was more discernible.

Since that time on Chatham Street, when he had been angry at Niresh, Amrith had promised himself that, if Niresh brought up the past again, he would try to tell him some things, like the story of his grandfather's cruelty to his mother. Yet, when the opportunity came up now, he had sensed the darkness opening up in him and he had been terrified.

Later that night, Amrith dreamt of the estate, of finding his mother's chair empty. He woke with a gasp and sat up.

"Had a nightmare?" Niresh murmured sleepily. He turned towards him and rested his hand on Amrith's back. "It's alright."

Amrith lay down, curled away from his cousin. He could not shake off the feeling of fear. There was a movement of sheets and then Niresh's hand slipped around his shoulder. "You're awake now, Amrith, it's alright. Just go to sleep, okay."

He could smell Niresh's breath against his shoulder, faintly sour like old milk.

His cousin had fallen asleep again, his breathing regular. Amrith, however, was wide-awake. He could feel the rise and fall of Niresh's chest against his back, the heat of his thighs resting against the back of his own. Amrith's penis had sprung up and he was afraid that his cousin's hand would move down accidentally and brush against it. But Niresh loosened his grip on Amrith and rolled over on his back with a sigh.

After a while, Amrith turned around, propped himself up on his elbow, and gazed at his cousin. His hair was disarranged over his forehead, his mouth slightly open, his lips glistening. Niresh's T-shirt was bunched up, exposing the rise and fall of his stomach, the hairs that fanned out from his navel.

When he was sure that Niresh was sound asleep, Amrith lay down on his back, as close to him as he dared. He moved his leg until his thigh was resting against his cousin's. He turned his head to the side so he could gaze at Niresh. After a while, so much heat had spread through Amrith's body that he seemed to be burning up with fever.

# 13

# Birthday Errands

~~~~~~~

**N**iresh settled into the routine of their lives and, within a day or two, it felt as if he had always lived with them.

Amrith was aware that his cousin, in order to keep Aunty Bundle and Uncle Lucky's good opinion of him, resisted smoking in the house, even though it caused him to fidget a lot – his fingers drumming on the surface of tables, bedposts, or pillars; his knees jiggling up and down when he was seated. The only time he smoked now was when they went on an excursion somewhere, or were down on the beach.

Amrith found that he did have to share his cousin with Selvi and her friends, especially when they were at the club. Yet, he was pleased that Niresh did not horse around as much with the girls anymore.

The girls were terribly disappointed. They complained

that he wasn't fun and tried to provoke him to chase them, to have water fights.

The girls also liked to make fun of his Canadian accent.

"Niresh, Niresh, say 'herbs'."

"'Erbs."

"Niresh, Niresh, say 'water'."

"Watrrr."

"Niresh, pronounce s-c-h-e-d-u-l-e."

"Skedule."

The girls would shriek with laughter, every time he replied.

Amrith could tell that his cousin was annoyed at this. It surprised him that Niresh was sensitive about his accent. Amrith thought it very glamorous, as did the girls really, despite their teasing. To all of them, Niresh sounded like someone from a Hollywood movie and Amrith had even begun to use some of his cousin's expressions, saying "yeah," instead of "yes."

He learned the reason for Niresh's sensitivity when he took him to visit Aunt Wilhelmina.

The old lady had been asking to see Niresh, but Amrith had avoided taking him over. He was worried how Aunt Wilhelmina would treat him. She remained incensed at his uncle for trying to sell Sanasuma, and he feared that she might vent her anger on Niresh.

By the third day of Niresh's stay with them, Amrith felt he could no longer postpone the visit. Yet, he felt it best to

warn his cousin, mostly because he was afraid that Niresh
might retaliate with rudeness and lose the good opinion of
Uncle Lucky and Aunty Bundle. Impoliteness to an old
person was unacceptable in Sri Lanka, no matter how
trying the provocation.

Once Amrith had got dressed for the visit, he sat on the
edge of his bed. "Niresh, I . . . I have to talk to you about
something."

Niresh was combing his hair and he turned away from
the mirror, worried by his tone.

Amrith picked at the coverlet. "Aunt Wilhelmina . . .
she might already dislike you."

"Because of my father?"

Amrith was surprised, as he often was, at how percep-
tive his cousin could be. "It's more than that."

Niresh came and sat by him and Amrith told him about
the sale of Sanasuma.

When he was done, Niresh got up and went to stand at
the French windows. After a moment, he thumped the
window frame hard. "Fuck." He turned to Amrith. "It's not
fair. That property should be yours."

Amrith looked at his hands.

Niresh stood in front of him. "Have you seen this
Sanasuma?"

"*Um* . . . yes."

"What does it look like?"

Amrith wanted to say that he did not wish to talk
about it but, instead, he found himself describing how the
bungalow was perched on a shelf of land, the mountains

all around it; how the stream tumbled into a rock pool.

"It sounds beautiful." Niresh sighed. "What does Sanasuma mean?"

"It's a Sinhalese word for a feeling of comfort or solace."

Later, as they left the bedroom, it struck Amrith that, while he had been telling Niresh about Sanasuma, he had not felt that familiar darkness opening up in him.

The visit to Aunt Wilhelmina's turned out as Amrith had predicted, and he was very glad he had warned his cousin. They arrived before the old lady's bridge game and the four dowagers were all seated in a row on the veranda, ensconced in Planter's chairs. Poor Niresh had to stand in front of them and be examined and questioned. Aunt Wilhelmina's friends had taken up Amrith's cause and so they, too, were unkind to Niresh. The old ladies talked about him as if he were not present, commenting on his height, his skin color, the length of his hair, his clothes, but especially on his accent, which they said sounded like those "dreadful American soldiers stationed here during the war." Niresh had been patient with them until this point, but when they started in on his accent, his eyes flashed with anger. Fortunately, the visit ended at this point. Ramu wheeled out the tea-trolley, which was always a sign for the ladies to take their places around the bridge table.

When they got into the car, Niresh was still furious. Finally he cried out, "Shit, I hate my accent."

"But, Niresh, why? You sound so great, like someone in a movie."

Niresh leaned back in his seat and looked out of the window. "It's just that when people comment on my accent, it makes we aware that I'm not Sri Lankan. I mean, I'm not Canadian and then, over here, I'm not Sri Lankan. I don't belong anywhere."

〰〰〰

The girls' birthday party was now four weeks away. That evening, the family sat together in the courtyard to draw up a final guest list, based on who had accepted invitations. They calculated 110 or 111 people, depending on whether Aunt Wilhelmina came to dinner or visited in the afternoon to give the girls their gifts. Amrith noticed that Niresh looked at them oddly, every time they added an adult to the list.

When they were going to dinner, Niresh said to Amrith, in an undertone, "So how come your aunt and uncle's friends are coming to the party?"

Amrith raised his eyebrows and shrugged. It was perfectly normal that they would.

Niresh smiled and shook his head. "Man, things are sure different here. Back in Canada, if your dad and mum had their friends to your birthday, you'd be considered a real loser."

With the party drawing nearer, the family began to worry even more about the hole in the roof, and if it would get fixed in time. Aunty Bundle sent her driver to remind the roofers, but when he got to their village, he found that Gineris and his sons were not even there. They had gone to repair roofs along the southern coast, in the towns of Matara and Galle. Gineris' wife did not know when he would be back, yet she assured them that her husband had not forgotten their roof and that he would soon be coming to Colombo to do a number of roofs that had been damaged by the monsoon.

When Uncle Lucky, Amrith, and the girls heard this, they began to have serious doubts that the roof would be done in time for the party. Uncle Lucky decided to act. He waited until Aunty Bundle was outstation, working on a hotel with Lucien Lindamulagé, and he got a roofer in Colombo to come and fix the problem.

Amrith and Niresh had gone along with Aunty Bundle, and they returned home that evening to find that the tub in the living room had been removed and there was no longer a gaping hole, open to the elements. When Aunty Bundle saw the repair, her mouth tightened in a thin line. "I hope you know what you're doing, Lucky," she said to her husband, who had come into the living room to stand by her. "I hope you haven't wasted your time and caused some further damage to the roof."

"Nonsense, Bundle," Uncle Lucky said, gesturing up to the rafters, "it looks as good as new."

"I am not so certain about that." She squinted up at it. "Those tiles don't look properly laid."

"There is no difference between them and the other tiles on the roof," Uncle Lucky replied, with a touch of impatience. "You are just imagining it."

"Well, let's see how they hold up when it next rains," Aunty Bundle said.

That very evening it did rain hard and the tiles held up fine. Uncle Lucky, who had a sense of humor behind his severe facade, could not help giving his wife little amused glances as they had dinner, the rain clattering on the roof above them. Aunty Bundle pretended not to notice him.

~~~~~~

Amrith still had a few days before rehearsals began and he was keen to have as much fun as possible with Niresh in the interim. They often ran errands with Aunty Bundle. His cousin was deeply drawn to her. Amrith would often observe him looking at her with hunger in his eyes. Niresh also found the places she went – places that were ordinary to Amrith – exotic. He frequently asked her questions about Sri Lankan habits and customs, and she was happy to draw on her vast knowledge to provide the answers. Amrith did not mind sharing Niresh with his aunt. She was an adult and so was no serious threat for his cousin's attention.

One morning, they accompanied her to order food and supplies for the party. First they went to Kumaran Stores.

When they entered the shop, Niresh looked around, intrigued. A long counter ran the length of the front. On one side, the customers jostled into each other as they called out their purchases to the clerks on the other side – who ran nimbly up and down ladders, moved deftly around gunnysacks that were brimming with cloves, cardamoms, dried chilies, and a dozen varieties of rice. The clerks weighed produce on scales, wrapped them in newspaper, tied the parcels with string from bolts that hung down from the ceiling, and wrote out receipts. The air was pungent with the odor of spices, curry powders, dried salty Maldive fish, and a massive bar of Sunlight soap from which the clerks cut slices for customers. In the midst of all this chaos, the mudalali, who owned the store, sat cross-legged on a bench, as bald and fat and serene as a Buddha. He wore a white sarong, and there was a red pottu and ash on his forehead. The cashbox was in front of him.

When he saw Aunty Bundle, he crocked his finger at a clerk, who lifted up a part of the front counter and invited Aunty Bundle, Amrith, and Niresh through. The mudalali gestured for them to be seated and, immediately, a tray with tea and soft drinks was presented to them. After a few pleasantries, they got down to business. Aunty Bundle ordered 15 pounds of Bombay onions for the seeni sambal and onion sambal, 20 coconuts, three bags of Maldive fish, 200 eggs for the hoppers and godambas, chili powder, curry powder, green chilies, turmeric, mustard seeds, coconut oil, and 15 broiler chickens. All this would be delivered three days before the party.

Next Aunty Bundle took them to the meat section of the Wellawatte Market. The moment they entered, they covered their noses. The stench of raw meat was overwhelming and the air was filled with the heavy thud of cleavers and wooden mallets falling against butcher blocks, the shrill cries of chickens as their necks were placed on a chopping block that had a drain underneath. They had to step around pools of blood, bits of gut, spleen, fat, and gristle that were all thickly covered with flies. Aunty Bundle placed a large order with her butcher for 20 pounds of beef, which would be needed for the curry.

Their final stops were Perera and Sons to order two birthday cakes and 250 patties, then they went around the corner to Bombay Sweet Mart to buy bags of Mixture filled with fried sticks of dough and cashews and chickpeas mixed with salt and chili powder. Here Niresh was introduced to the pleasure of faluda, a rose-flavored milkshake, with bits of semolina floating in it, and crisply fried samosas.

Amrith needed a new shirt for the party. He and Niresh drove with Aunty Bundle to the bustling bazaars of Pettah. As they drew near, Aunty Bundle said, "Now, Niresh, we are about to enter the oldest section of Colombo, which was settled in the seventeenth century by the Dutch colonizers, who were my ancestors." Niresh leaned forward, listening, as Aunty Bundle continued on. "The word 'Pettah' is an Anglo-Indian word and comes from the Tamil expression 'Pettai,' which was used in India to describe a suburb outside a fort."

They were approaching Pettah from a route they did not usually take and Aunty Bundle suddenly exclaimed, "*Ah,* here we are." She indicated for her driver, Mendis, to stop. She rolled down her car window and beckoned for

Niresh to lean forward and look out. "Over there are the last remaining Dutch houses." She was pointing to a row of one-storied houses with tiled roofs that slanted down sharply and were pitched low over a deep veranda. The roofs were supported by slim wooden or brick pillars. The verandas were raised a few feet above the street, and a wooden railing ran along the edge of them. The houses were in a terrible state, some of the verandas falling apart, the walls with green rot climbing up the side of them.

Aunty Bundle grimaced. "There is little effort to preserve houses like these. In our two thousand-year-old civilization, something from the seventeenth century seems so new. We are a poor country and there isn't enough money to keep up the ancient monuments and these as well."

She pointed out features of the houses, explaining to Niresh how this house style was adapted by Sri Lankans. She showed him the details of the massive framed doors, with heavily paneled shutters and the equally lofty windows on either side. Though they were not going to go in, she laid out for him the interior of the house. When one entered, there was a long narrow passage, from which doors led into the bedrooms. It ended at the zaal (which became "saleya" in Sinhalese) – a wide and lofty room stretching nearly the whole breadth of the house, which was the eating and living room of the family. Beyond the zaal was the back veranda.

Once she had finished her description, they drove on for a bit and then, because they were entering the oldest parts of Pettah, where the roads were very narrow, Mendis parked the car and they continued on foot.

As they hurried through the congested streets, Amrith noticed how fascinated his cousin was by the thick press of people, the hawkers calling out their wares from the makeshift pavement stalls. There was a smell of mothballs and incense in the air mixed with the aroma of teas, spices, ayurvedic medicinal balms, and frying food from the snack stands. A lorry carrying chickens blasted its horn as it tried to maneuver its way through the pedestrians who took up the streets.

Aunty Bundle and Amrith were used to the sights and smells and they hurried along, but they kept losing Niresh and retracing their steps to get him. He had noticed a snake charmer, who was tempting him to pay for a show by lifting the lid of his woven basket so Niresh could see the cobra lying inside. Then Niresh joined a crowd around a couple of performing monkeys, which were dressed as a man and a woman and were enacting a lewd tale, narrated by their master. The male spectators were grinning and hooting; the women pressing their handkerchiefs or sari palus to their mouths in a pretense of modesty, but really to hide their titters.

When they finally arrived at Kundanmal's, where Aunty Bundle was a regular customer, they were immediately attended to.

The clerk led them to a counter and, from glass-fronted cabinets on the wall, he drew out the rolls of fabric that

Amrith pointed to, and flung them with practiced flair along the counter, bolt upon bolt upon bolt. Amrith had a photograph of the shirt he wanted made, torn out of an old American teen magazine he had found at a bookstall on Maradana Road.

Niresh grimaced as Amrith laid it on the counter. "That's a bit out of date," he said, "too disco."

"What do you suggest, then?"

Niresh narrowed his eyes at the bolts of fabric in the cabinet and pointed to a material that was not shiny like the ones Amrith had chosen. The clerk spun the cloth out over the counter saying, "Good choice, sir, very new." It was a fairly somber blue, with white stripes.

Aunty Bundle was waiting and Amrith nodded to say he would get it. The clerk began to put the other bolts of fabric away.

"*Uh,* do you think I could have a shirt made, too?" Niresh asked, turning to Aunty Bundle.

"But why, dear? You have such nice shirts in Canada. Ours must seem so homemade by comparison."

"I've never had a shirt made just for me."

She smiled. "Which material would you like?"

He pointed to a green version of Amrith's fabric. "Do you mind?"

"No, no, not at all." Amrith was thrilled that they would have matching shirts.

When the clerk had cut the two materials and put them in a brown paper bag, he began to write out a receipt.

"I'll pay for my own." Niresh reached for his wallet.

"Definitely not, dear." Aunty Bundle indicated to the clerk to put everything on one bill. "This is my gift to you. Something to remember us by."

Niresh smiled and thanked her.

The tailor needed to be summoned to sew the shirts. He was a tiny wizened man they called Cut-and-Put because he would say to Aunty Bundle, in the poor English he insisted on speaking with her, "Lady, we must cut-and-put the dress like this," or, "Lady, it is not fashionable to cut-and-put in that way."

His clothes were always a very good fit, though the inside seams were done messily and so, invariably, the garments would have to be dispatched to another tailor to be tidied up.

Aunty Bundle sent a note with her driver to Cut-and-Put: *Tailor, please come immediately. Urgent sewing needed. Mrs. Manuel-Pillai.*

He turned up the next morning. They were at breakfast, when Jane-Nona brought him in. He was bent over with age, and wore thick glasses and a polyester safari suit. He came towards them, holding out the note. "Lady, you have called for me?"

Once Aunty Bundle had greeted him and inquired after his family, Jane-Nona took him to the kitchen for a cup of tea.

When he had gone, Aunty Bundle turned to Amrith and Niresh. "Now, you boys, please stay home this morning.

Go by often and give him lots of praise. He's terribly tem-
peramental and touchy." She shook her head. "Oh, dear, he's
so fussy about lunch. Jane! Jane-Nona!"

When she came out, Aunty Bundle said in a hushed
tone, "Check with him before you cook; you know how
he is."

"I already did, missie." She smiled. "Evidently, he's only
eating fish these days. Seer fish, at that." They looked at
each other and giggled.

"Well, I guess we should be grateful it's not prawns or
crabs," Aunty Bundle said.

"Yes, missie, or some vegetable that is out of season."

Niresh had done a rough drawing of a shirt so Cut-and-
Put could see that now the collar lapels were narrower
than they were a few years ago during the height of disco,
and that shirts were looser fitting. His cousin was skepti-
cal that Cut-and-Put would be able to sew a shirt from
such a rough sketch, but Cut-and-Put glanced at Niresh's
sketch, asked him a couple of questions, and then began
to measure him.

Cut-and-Put set himself up in the living room on a mat,
in front of the sewing machine that had belonged to Aunty
Bundle's mother. The shirts would be done in a few hours, as
he worked fast. Amrith and Niresh came by to duly praise
him. He seemed taken with Niresh and said to him,
"Young-master, I will make better shirt than from Canada."

When they had their first fitting, the pins gently sticking into their bodies, he said, "See young-master, better

than imported, I make." And Amrith and Niresh agreed, with an amused glance at each other.

When the tailor was done, the boys stood next to each other in the mirror, looking at their reflections. They smiled to acknowledge that they liked wearing matching shirts.

Yet, Amrith also felt sad. His cousin would not be here to wear his new shirt at the birthday party. He would return to Canada a few days beforehand.

# 14

# Amrith's Troubles

~~~~~~~
~~~~~~~

The afternoon before rehearsals began, Amrith and Niresh returned from errands with Aunty Bundle to find a meeting of the Catholic Students' Union in progress in the court-yard. Suraj was present and he sat with his hands clasped to his breast, his head bent, a pious look on his face, as he fervently recited the rosary along with the others. Amrith could not help grinning at his devout expression, clearly meant to impress Mala, who was leading the rosary.

Niresh was standing by the car, gaping. He leaned close to Amrith. "What kind of freak show is this?"

Amrith was half-shocked, half-titillated. He told Niresh what was going on, surprised that he knew nothing about the rosary, even though he must have been baptized a Catholic.

They went to their bedroom. As they passed the group, Suraj, even though he was supposed to be praying, followed Niresh with his eyes. He frowned when Mala smiled at

Niresh, while she waited for the others to say the second part of the Hail Mary.

In the bedroom, as Niresh sat in a chair and began to remove his shoes and socks, he said, "Who's the guy with the single eyebrow?"

Amrith giggled. Suraj's eyebrows were so thick they met in the middle, forming a continuous line. He would never have thought to comment on this irregularity, as Suraj was revered in school.

"So," Niresh said, tilting his head to one side, "uni-brow has the hots for Mala."

Amrith nodded, grinning. He found this budding romance very amusing, and he told Niresh how Mala, since she realized that Suraj was interested in her, had taken to saying little coy, flirty things to him whenever they met. Suraj was delighted by these exchanges.

"*In*-teresting." Niresh threw his shoes into a corner and put on his rubber slippers. "Will he make the moves on her?"

Amrith shook his head. "Suraj would not dare cross that line because our families know each other well."

Niresh grabbed his arm. "Hey, let's go by them again."

He led the way out of the bedroom. Amrith followed, excited to see what mischief his cousin had in mind. Mala had finished her half of a Hail Mary and the other students were reciting the second half, their heads bent. She looked up at Amrith and Niresh as they passed by. His cousin grabbed his chest, crossed his eyes, stuck out his tongue, and made his legs buckle. Mala snuffled and quickly bent her head. Amrith and Niresh ran towards the living room, giggling. Suraj had turned to watch them and, before he went in, Niresh gave him a cool look.

"Hey, let's do something else," Niresh said, when they were in the living room.

"Yes." Amrith looked around and saw a broom. "Why don't you pretend to be Christ on the cross and I'll pretend to be Mary Magdalene weeping at your feet?" He was delighted by his own daring, his blasphemy.

"Good idea." Niresh grabbed the broom and laid it across his shoulders. They waited until they heard Mala's voice reciting her half of the Hail Mary and they took their positions in the doorway. Niresh stood with his arms outstretched, a pious look of suffering on his face, his eyes rolled to heaven. Amrith knelt at his feet, his hands clasped, looking up at him adoringly, but with half an eye on his sister.

Mala finished. She glanced up, saw them, and gave a small cry of surprise, which she quickly turned into a cough. She bent her head in prayer, her shoulders shaking with laughter.

Amrith and Niresh darted back inside, giggling.

The students had finished the last decades of the rosary and they began to recite the creed together. The moment they were done, Mala stood up and hurried to the living room. Niresh and Amrith were waiting for her.

"Stop it, you boys, stop it." She was laughing so hard, she had to hold her stomach.

Amrith tried to tickle her and she shrieked and ran into the pantry. When they found her, she was pouring out passion fruit cordial into glasses on a tray.

"Hey, let me bring that out," Niresh said, when the drinks were ready. He tried to pick up the tray.

"Certainly not." Mala placed her hand on it. "This is a serious meeting."

"Come on. I promise to be nice." He moved the tray away from her.

"No!" She made a grab for it, but Niresh held it out of reach.

Jane-Nona was watching all this with interest, from the kitchen.

Niresh took the tray to the pantry door and pushed it open for Mala. He bowed. "After you, madam."

"Oh, what is this, men?" Mala cried with false exasperation as she went out.

Amrith followed, grinning. He was sure Niresh was going to do something funny.

As his cousin passed around the tray, he bowed before each person, calling them madam or sir. The girls were amused and charmed, but the boys were not. Particularly Suraj, who glared at Niresh. When he reached Suraj, he held out the tray. "A drink for you, madam. Oh, sorry, I mean sir."

Mala giggled and, though Suraj tried to take the joke in good form, he was furious.

~~~~~
~~~~~

When Amrith stood before the school gates the next morning, he knew he was unprepared for this rehearsal. It had been over three weeks since he had memorized his lines for the audition and he had forgotten most of them.

Last evening, he had intended to run through his part with Niresh but, instead, they had lain on the bed, chatting away about various things, the copy of *Othello* open between them. Time had passed rapidly, as it always did when they were talking, and, just as Amrith was finally insisting that they must pay attention and run through lines, Aunty Bundle had knocked on their bedroom door and asked them to turn the lights off.

With a sigh, Amrith pushed open the school gate and went up the front path. Not only was he worried about being unprepared, but he was also loath to spend the morning away from Niresh.

When Amrith came into the auditorium, he found the boys seated around Fernando, who was conducting a quick line rehearsal before Madam arrived. "*Ah,* De Alwis," he said, beckoning him forward, "let's start at the beginning and run through your part, too."

Amrith swallowed hard as he went to sit beside Fernando. Now that he was actually here, his failure to learn his lines was more serious than it had seemed this morning at breakfast. None of the other boys had their copies of *Othello* open. Peries was present and, when Amrith happened to meet his eye, he looked away.

Suraj began Othello's opening monologue, his eyes closed in concentration, Fernando prompting him every so often. Amrith surreptitiously opened his book and glanced at his lines. He read the first one over and over again, hoping that by knowing it, the rest would return to him spontaneously.

He was paying so much attention to his task that he did not realize Suraj had come to the end of his monologue. He glanced up to find that the other boys were staring at him.

"De Alwis." Fernando reached over and shut Amrith's copy of *Othello*. "Give us your first line."

The moment the book closed, Amrith could not even remember the line he had looked at just now. The others were waiting. "*Um . . . um . . .* cue, please," he said, softly.

"*Who's . . .*" Fernando prompted.

"*Who's there?*"

Fernando nodded, but then indicated with his hand that there was more.

"*Um . . . who's there? Othello?*"

"Good-good." Fernando gestured to Suraj, who said, "*Ay, Desdemona.*" Fernando indicated to Amrith, who looked at him blankly and finally said, "Cue?"

"*Will . . .*" Fernando prompted.

"*Will . . . will . . . will.*" Amrith could not remember.

There was a rustle of feigned impatience from Peries. He called out, in a bored voice, "*Will you come to bed, my lord?*"

"*Will you come to bed, my lord?*" Amrith scowled at his rival, who smirked back at him.

"*Have you prayed tonight, Desdemona?*" Suraj continued.

Again, Amrith did not know what to say and Peries chimed in, "*Ay, my lord.*"

*"If you bethink yourself of any crime*
*Unreconciled as yet to heaven and grace,*
*Solicit for it straight."* Suraj was now addressing himself to Peries.

*"Alack, my lord, what may you mean by that?"* Peries replied.

The two of them began to volley lines back and forth, Peries thoroughly enjoying showing Amrith up, a triumphant gleam in his eyes.

When Peries and Suraj came to the end of their exchange, there was clapping from the back of the auditorium. The boys spun around. Madam was standing by the door. She had probably been there quite a while. Amrith felt a sinking within.

Madam came briskly down the aisle. "Okay, let's set up the scene."

The boys rose from their seats. Amrith got up to follow them, but Madam called his name. She beckoned for him to follow her out of the auditorium, indicating that Fernando should come along, too.

When they were outside, she turned to Amrith. "De Alwis, what is going on? Didn't you learn your lines?"

"I . . . I did, Madam. I've just not practiced them in a while. I meant to run through lines last night, but I didn't have a chance."

"That's not good enough, De Alwis," Madam said, severely.

"I . . . I know, Madam." But then wishing to justify his lapse, he said, "My cousin is visiting from Canada and so

I've had to show him around and there hasn't been much time for anything else."

"Make the time, De Alwis, make the time," said Fernando, frowning at him. "This is important; you can't let down the school colors."

"I'll accept your excuse this time." Madam patted him on the arm. "You've always been very conscientious."

He nodded gratefully.

"But I want you to stay out here and learn your lines." She raised her eyebrows as he looked at her, dismayed. "I'll send one of the boys who is playing a courtier or some other supernumerary to run through lines with you."

Amrith hung his head. Peries would be taking his place today.

He spent the next hour practicing and, when he was confident he had his lines down, he went back into the auditorium. He made sure to sit where Madam could see him. She noted his presence, but did not invite him to replace Peries onstage. Amrith watched his rival with hatred. Peries was really showing off, taking advantage of Amrith's lapse.

Amrith's only consolation was that Madam did not make him play the part of Cassio. Instead, when they got to that point in the scene, she called on Peries to get off the bed – where he lay pretending to be the murdered Desdemona – and assume his role.

Amrith, with nothing to do, kept glancing at a clock on the stage wall, dismayed at how slowly time was passing. He found himself wondering what Niresh was doing and he felt a longing, like homesickness, rise in him. He ached to be with his cousin again, to see his face, to sit in his company. How interminably far away twelve o'clock seemed.

Niresh had planned to come and pick him up after the rehearsal. As Amrith walked down to the gates with Madam and the other students, he saw the car waiting outside and quickened his pace.

When he came out of the gates, the door opened and Niresh stepped out. "Hey, buddy!"

Amrith felt a rush of joy. "Hi!" he cried back.

Niresh put his arm around his shoulder and gave him a hug. Amrith blushed with pleasure.

"De Alwis."

He turned. Madam and Fernando had been watching. The other boys had scattered to the cars that were waiting for them and to the bicycle shed. Suraj, however, lingered, glowering at Niresh.

"*Ah,* De Alwis, is this the relative from abroad who's keeping you from learning your lines?" There was a touch of amusement in Madam's voice.

Amrith hastily made the introduction.

As she shook Niresh's hand, she looked him over, then glanced at Fernando. "Well, yes, De Alwis, I can see why you have been distracted and haven't had time for our little play." She patted him on the arm. "I'm *sure* you'll enjoy the rest of your afternoon, De Alwis." She gestured to Fernando and they wandered off together, smiling.

Amrith saw that Suraj had seen their amusement. He got into the car feeling strangely uncomfortable.

~~~~~
~~~~~

Amrith's bad day got worse when he reached home. In his absence, he found out that Niresh and the girls had made arrangements for all of them to see a film that afternoon, at the Majestic. His cousin's treat. When Niresh told him about the plan at lunch, Amrith was careful not to let his anger show. He felt the girls glancing anxiously at him and he refused to meet their eyes.

Because he was not used to the heat, Niresh was always exhausted by midday and often fell into a deep slumber when the family lay down after lunch. That afternoon, Amrith waited to make sure his cousin was properly asleep, then he quietly put on his rubber slippers and tiptoed out of the French windows. He made his way across the side garden to the girls' room.

He entered to find them lying on their beds, reading some out-of-date teen magazines.

They glanced at him, then gave each other a quick look.

"Amrith, we wanted to explain –" Mala began apologetically, but Selvi cut her short.

"There's nothing to explain, Mala. We didn't do anything wrong." Selvi flipped the pages of her magazine.

"I told you both not to make any plans with my cousin. I thought we agreed on that." Amrith, because of his humiliation this morning, was angrier than he would have normally been.

"We didn't make the plans." Selvi threw down her magazine and picked up another one.

"Then who did?" he demanded.

She raised her eyebrows at him. "Who do you think? Niresh."

He glanced at Mala and she nodded to confirm this was so.

"I . . . I don't believe you," he said, lamely.

"Ask him yourself, then." Selvi smiled at him. "Niresh invited me."

"You're lying. You probably hinted so much that he had no choice but to stand you a film. Haven't you any shame – are you a beggar?"

Selvi lifted her chin. "Maybe Niresh is sick of constantly being with you. He is, after all, two years older, my age, and probably wants some sophisticated company rather than the companionship of a child."

Amrith was furious. He strode to her bed, but then stood by it helplessly.

"Akka," Mala said, trying to smooth things over. "Don't lie. Niresh did not even ask you first. I was the one he asked." She held her arms out to Amrith. "But, of course, he asked if I would like to come with you both. He honestly did. He mentioned you in the same breath as himself."

She was offering him her support, but Amrith rejected it with a toss of his head. "*Ah!* So now you're also throwing yourself at him."

Mala flushed with hurt.

He glared at both of them. "I don't want either of you to come."

"Oh? And what excuse should we give Niresh?" Selvi demanded. "Perhaps we should tell him the truth. That his cousin is a jealous baby."

"I don't care. Just don't come. The both of you." He glanced at Mala, who looked away. She was angry with him now.

"If you don't want us to come, you can make up the excuse," Selvi said, starting to read her magazine again. "I'm going to be ready at three thirty, unless I hear otherwise. Now get out of our room."

Amrith stormed out and went up to the terrace. Yet it was too hot at this time of the afternoon for him to be there long. He soon returned to his bedroom and lay on his bed, fuming.

Part of the reason the sisters refused to bow out of the plan was because they were going to see *Grease,* which had finally reached Sri Lanka two years after it had opened in the West. Selvi and Mala had been looking forward to the film, as they were fans of Olivia Newton-John. Uncle Lucky had bought them the soundtrack to *Grease* on one of his trips abroad, and they knew all the songs by heart. Yet they could not go to the film unchaperoned. Sri Lankan cinemas were notorious for perverted men, who, in the dark, attempted all manner of indecencies on unescorted girls. Many women carried a pin or a needle to repel offenders.

When they all gathered in the courtyard at three thirty, Amrith saw that Selvi and Mala were grimly determined to enjoy this occasion. Niresh had, of course, seen the movie when it opened in Canada and, as they walked up their street towards Galle Road, he teased the girls by threatening to reveal plot points. They shrieked at him to keep quiet and mock-threatened that they would not sit with him in the cinema, as he was sure to spoil the movie for them. He began to sing "Hopelessly Devoted to You" in a silly senti-mental manner, holding his arms out to the girls. They were on busy Galle Road by now and pedestrians turned to stare at Niresh's antics, some men grinning and calling out encouragement to him in Sinhalese. The girls were half-amused, half-mortified, and they scuttled ahead of Niresh, giggling to each other and saying things like, "*Aiyo,* Mala, look at this boy, he's shaming us, *nah*," and "Yes-yes, akka. *Aiyo,* I hope Aunt Wilhelmina or one of her friends doesn't pass by and see this. We will be in big-big trouble."

Amrith trailed behind all of them, ignored.

By the time they reached the cinema, Amrith was seething. As they stood in line to buy the tickets, the others paid him no attention as a fairly earnest tussle began to develop between Niresh and the girls over his paying for them.

"No-no, Niresh," Selvi insisted, with a slight haughti-ness that was intended for Amrith, "we are not beggars. We are quite capable of buying our own tickets." She took out a twenty-rupee bill from her purse as they drew nearer to the ticket kiosk.

"Yeah, but I want to," Niresh replied, grinning. "You guys have been so nice to me, it's the least I can do."

"No, no, absolutely not," Mala murmured.

They were at the kiosk now and Niresh pushed Selvi's hand away and told the agent not to take their money. Mala, however, snatched the twenty-rupee bill away from her sister and held it out to the agent. Before he could take it, Niresh grabbed her hand and lowered it. Still holding on to her hand, he pushed his money through the opening in the glass and ordered the tickets.

Niresh wanted to buy snacks from the refreshment stand and he needed someone to help him. He asked Amrith to accompany him and told the girls they would meet them in the cinema. Amrith was pleased to be selected and he gave the girls a triumphant look as he went with his cousin.

Niresh was intrigued by the snacks that were available, which were completely different from what you got at a Canadian cinema. He was particularly surprised that there was no popcorn. Niresh bought a lot of things – icy chocs, packets of deviled cashews, banana chips, paper cones of fried spiced dhal, bars of Kandos chocolate. He also wanted to try the various pop drinks that he had never heard of before, like Portello and Fanta and Necto.

Armed with all these snacks, they went into the theater. Mala and Selvi were sitting in the middle of a row and Amrith hurried a little ahead of his cousin, determined to seat himself between Niresh and the girls. As he took his place, he saw the look of disappointment on his cousin's face. He felt both angry and downcast. Nobody seemed to want him here at all.

Niresh soon adjusted to this arrangement and he began to talk to the girls across Amrith, who was forced to lean back in his seat so a conversation could be carried on in front of him. Even when the film began, Niresh periodically leaned over him to say something to Mala, who was seated next to Amrith.

By the end of the film, Amrith was livid.

# 15

# Betrayal

~~~~~~
~~~~~~

**S**elvi soon forgot the fight. She had got what she wanted, which was to see *Grease*. Mala, however, had not forgiven Amrith, though he was no longer angry at them. He became aware of her feelings the next day, when he asked her to run through lines with him and she coldly refused, saying she had other things to do. He was puzzled. Usually she forgave him even greater misdeeds, like revealing her secret wish to be a nun. His accusation, that she had thrown herself at Niresh, seemed to have stung in a more lasting way.

That evening, when the family sat out in the courtyard, Amrith and the girls introduced Niresh to Carom, a board-game version of billiards. He was instantly intrigued by it and, once the rules had been explained, he was eager to try the game. Selvi found Carom boring and she excused herself and went to talk with one of her friends on the phone.

Amrith was terrible at the game, but Mala was an expert. No one in the family had beaten her, so far. It was she who showed Niresh how to play, and she often put her hand over his to guide him in a particular move. They began to tease each other, Niresh vowing that he would beat Mala, she replying, with a superior smirk, that she looked forward to that day. They laughed out loud and clapped their hands in exultation when they knocked each other's piece into the net.

Amrith was soon out of the game and he sat watching, trying to stifle his irritation as the competition between them grew fierce and they forgot his presence altogether.

At one point, he noticed Mala looking at him. She had sensed his irritation. Yet, rather than withdrawing and leaving him alone with his cousin, she looked away, as if his feelings no longer mattered to her.

The next evening, when they were at the club, Niresh changed quicker than Amrith because he did not wait for a curtained cubicle to come free. He left the dressing room when he was done, telling Amrith he would meet him by the pool.

After Amrith had put on his trunks, he went looking for Niresh and saw him sitting at one end of the garden, talking to Mala. She was in her bathing costume, seated on a lounge chair, a book open on her lap. As Amrith made his

way towards Niresh, the SNOTs and Selvi approached
his cousin, crying, "Niresh, Niresh, what is this, men? Just
sitting and talking like a real boring type. Aren't you going
to swim? How about a game of water polo?"

He smiled, but continued talking to Mala.

Then one of the girls cried, "Are you interested in Mala,
or something?"

Niresh blushed.

"He is, he is!" they shrieked. "Mala, did you see, you
have a boyfriend!"

Mala smiled, slipped down on the lounger, and held her
book in front of her face.

Niresh leapt off his chair and, with a war cry, charged
after the girls. They screamed and ran away from him –
towards the pool, of course. Niresh signaled to Amrith
and he joined reluctantly in the chase, the girls running
around the pool, allowing themselves to be cornered and
pushed in.

While this was going on, Amrith saw that Mala had
come to the edge of the pool. He sneaked up behind her
and, with a cry, rushed forward and pushed her into the
water. The next moment Niresh had pushed him over
the edge and leapt in too. He grinned and touched Amrith
on the shoulder.

Meanwhile, Mala had swum to a side of the pool.

"Oh-oh," Niresh said, grabbing Amrith's arm, "here
comes lover-boy."

Suraj Wanigasekera was making his way across the
garden. It was clear he was looking for Mala. When he saw

her in the pool, he squatted down to talk with her. Niresh winked at Amrith, then sank down underwater and swam silently towards Mala. When he reached her, he grabbed hold of her legs. She screamed as she went under, hit out at him, and broke away. She swam off laughing. Niresh did not follow. Instead, he stood up in the pool and grinned at Suraj. "Hi, how are you doing?"

Suraj glared at him and walked away.

Mala had noticed the exchange between the two boys, and there was an odd smile on her face. A terrible uneasiness began to take hold of Amrith.

There was a rehearsal the next morning. It was just for Amrith and Suraj to practice their scene together. Madam and Fernando were the only other people present.

The boys were in the wings, waiting for Madam and Fernando to finish a discussion about the costumes, when Suraj leaned close to Amrith. "So how is your dear cousin?" He raised his eyebrows.

Amrith shrugged and bent over his copy of *Othello*.

"Ni-resh," Suraj continued. "And is he leaving soon for Canada?"

Amrith looked up quickly, his eyes naked, the question bringing a pang of sadness to him.

Suraj snickered. "I guess you're going to really-really miss your cousin, *ah*."

At that moment, Madam called them to take their places.

As Amrith lay on the two benches that were pushed together to serve as a bed, he looked at Suraj doing his monologue and realized that he disliked him. He had been too cowed by Suraj's popularity to admit this to himself before.

That afternoon, when they were at lunch, Amrith found out that his cousin, instead of reading or going on errands with Aunty Bundle, had gone with Mala to the parish hall to help her teach English to slum children. As the family ate, Niresh told them about how cute the children were and how sorry he felt that they were so poor. He praised Mala, saying that she was a wonderful, patient teacher and the students all loved her. When he said this, he glanced at her almost anxiously. She nodded primly and changed the subject.

The girls had a fitting at the dressmaker's that evening, before going to the club. Niresh and Amrith went with them. The sisters both wanted the same style of dress, but in different colors – a copy of the outfit that John Travolta's girlfriend had worn for the dance competition in *Saturday Night Fever*, with a gathered skirt, a frill around the neckline, and a sleeve on only one shoulder. Selvi, because she was light-skinned, was getting the dress made in the same pink the actress had worn; Mala would get it in cream, which complemented her dark skin.

The dressmaker, Mrs. Spillars, had an aviary that was much grander than Amrith's, with parrots and cockatoos imported from Australia and an albino peacock. Amrith took Niresh to look at it.

They were leaning against the mesh, watching the birds, when Niresh put his arm around Amrith's shoulders. "Hey, can I tell you a secret?"

"Sure," Amrith said, eagerly.

Niresh looked at him and then away. "I think I'm in love." He gave Amrith a lopsided grin. "And guess who with? Mala."

Amrith felt a tightening in his throat.

"Yeah, I think she's really cute and really nice and –" Niresh caught himself short. "Hey, I hope you don't mind my talking about her like that."

"*Um* . . . no." Amrith was suddenly miserable. He saw now that he had been aware of his cousin's attraction over the last few days. He had just not admitted it to himself. It was also clear why Mala was cold towards him. She returned Niresh's feelings and felt guilty about it.

"I mean, you're my main man, my best buddy," Niresh continued, smiling sweetly at him. "You're the only one I could tell something like this to, *eh?*"

Amrith looked away at the birds in the aviary.

"So, do you think she fancies me?" Niresh asked.

"You? I don't think so."

Niresh punched him in the arm. "Yeah, I think."

"What about Suraj?"

"He's history."

"Don't be so cocky. She has known Suraj much longer than you."

"Anyways," Niresh said, "it's just between us, *eh*. I mean, I know the rule about you guys not dating until you're eighteen. I would never screw with that. Your aunt and uncle have been really nice to me. So I'm just telling you because you're my best buddy."

Amrith nodded, but he continued to stare into the aviary, a great heaviness building inside him.

Despite what Niresh had said about respecting the rule, when they were done at the dressmaker's and were walking towards the car, he kept step with Mala, talking to her. Amrith was left to trail behind with Selvi. Mala laughed at something Niresh said, and the sound of her laughter was like a gate clanging shut, leaving Amrith on the outside. Looking at his sister, he felt a bitter anger towards her. She had betrayed him.

<center>~~~~~</center>

The next morning Amrith had a rehearsal and, this time, he was even more disinclined to go. Niresh had said nothing about what he planned to do with his morning, but Amrith guessed he would go to the parish hall with Mala.

The rehearsal was for the whole cast, and all the actors were present. As Amrith waited in the wings, he was so distracted by the thought of what Niresh was doing that he did not hear Madam calling his name. Finally, one of the boys nudged him and he hurriedly went onstage and took his place on the bed.

Yet, even as he lay there, he could not stop thinking of Mala and Niresh together at the parish hall; he could not help remembering the way Mala had laughed at the dressmaker's and how it had sounded like a gate shutting in his face. Last evening, Mala and Niresh had played Carom again, and though Amrith had wanted to play Scrabble instead, his knowledge of their attraction to each other had silenced him.

"De Alwis!"

He came out of his reverie to find Madam standing at the front of the auditorium, by the stage.

"De Alwis, pay attention, for goodness' sake. Wanigasekera finished his monologue. Didn't you hear Fernando calling your cue?"

"*Um* . . . sorry, Madam."

Suraj said softly, "Daydreaming about your cousin?"

Amrith looked at him surprised, and Suraj laughed.

"Come on, boys," Madam called, "let's do it again."

Suraj took his place and went through his monologue once more. Amrith made sure to pay attention this time and, when it came to his cue, he began the dialogue between them.

He was barely a few lines into the scene, however, when Madam stopped him.

"For goodness' sake, De Alwis! Could you be any more unemotional? Your husband has just woken you to say he is going to murder you in your bed. From your nonchalance, one would think that he was offering you some trifling news."

"Sorry, Madam."

"Come-come, put some passion behind it – make it seem like you're really frightened."

Amrith's heart was not in this rehearsal, yet he knew what was at stake here. When they did the scene again, he forced himself to give the performance required of him, but it felt like physical exertion when one is sick.

Madam soon stopped him. "My, De Alwis! From one extreme to the other, *nah*. Now you are completely over-the-top. Almost a caricature."

She beckoned to him and he got off the bed and went to the edge of the stage. "De Alwis," she said, frowning, "if you are not able to give this role your attention, I am sure there are others who would be delighted to do so."

Peries, who was in the front row, sat up in his seat, looking expectantly at Madam. She ignored him. Once she had finished talking to Amrith and was going back down the aisle, Peries put up his hand.

"What is it, Peries?" Madam glanced at him, annoyed.

"I was wondering, Madam, if you want me to take De Alwis' place."

Amrith was outraged. Madam was not happy, either. "I am the director, Peries," she said, in a chilly voice, "I will decide when, if at all, that will happen."

Once rehearsals were over, Madam made Amrith stay behind. She waited until the other boys had left and then she turned to him with a gentle smile. "De Alwis, I really sense your heart isn't in this role, so I want to offer you the chance to bow out. I won't be angry at you. Sometimes a role is just not right for an actor, you know."

"No, Madam." Amrith looked at her pleadingly. "I . . . I promise I'll work hard at it."

"Is your Canadian cousin distracting you?"

Amrith looked away. "A little."

"Well, this is a warning. I have been very patient but, as you know, I must put the interest of the school ahead of everything else. This is a final warning, De Alwis."

He hung his head and nodded.

When Amrith came down to the gate, the car was there, but Niresh was not in it.

As the car turned down their road, Amrith saw Niresh and Mala. They were walking ahead, talking animatedly. His cousin was carrying Mala's bag. Niresh laughed at something she said and she punched him in the arm.

The car reached the gate at the same time they did. "Hey, buddy," Niresh cried out, as he went to drag back the gate so the car could enter. Mala hurried ahead and went into the house.

Amrith greeted Niresh as civilly as he could, before excusing himself and going to his room.

That afternoon, they were all supposed to go to the club, but Amrith insisted that he wanted to go down to Kinross Beach for a swim with his cousin. Niresh agreed reluctantly.

When they came out of the bedroom, on their way to Kinross, Mala was pacing aimlessly under the jak tree.

"Hey," Niresh said, crossing to her in delight. "Do you want to come with us?"

Mala tried to appear surprised at Niresh's invitation, but Amrith could tell that she had been hoping they would ask her.

Once she had gone to change, Niresh turned to Amrith. "You don't mind, do you?"

"No, of course not, why should I?" Amrith replied.


They had been in the water a short while when Mala walked back to the beach, spread her towel out, and sat down. Amrith was glad to see her go. Now he had his cousin all to himself.

After a moment, however, Niresh, without a word or glance at him, waded out to join her.

Amrith could have followed him and sat with them on the beach, but he stayed in the water, going under, trying to get a glimpse of the bottom. He searched for pretty shells. Occasionally he saw one but, before he could reach out to grab it, the sand shifted and it disappeared.

When he felt he had been in the water long enough to make a point he could not name, he walked casually up the beach to join them.

As he came towards them, Niresh was saying, "Yeah, it was hard. It was hard growing up without my mum. I really missed her all the time, at first." He turned over a strand of dried sea-weed, a sad expression on his face that did not look completely genuine. His cousin was appealing to Mala's ready sympathy, and she looked at him, her eyes luminous with pity.

Niresh had noticed Amrith approaching and a fleeting look of annoyance crossed his face. It pierced Amrith's heart.

# 16

## The Catholic Students' Union
## Does a Shramadana

〰〰〰〰
〰〰〰〰

The next day, the Catholic Students' Union met at an old folks' home to do a shramadana. Selvi and her friends were going along as well, and it turned out that other boys and girls, who were not in the Union, had volunteered their time for a chance to be around one another. When Niresh heard about the shramadana, he wanted to go. Amrith was not keen, but he agreed to accompany him. Since he had discovered Niresh and Mala's attraction to each other, he found it very difficult to assert his will and insist on time alone with his cousin.

The old folks' home, donated by a wealthy philanthropist, was in a large bungalow with a back and front veranda and an extensive garden. The majority of the residents were

Dutch Burghers. They were the last remnants of a racial group that was dying out rapidly in this country, their families having left for Australia, Canada, and England in the 1950s and 60s. Various Burgher associations in the West contributed generously to the upkeep of the home.

Neither the residents, who were for the most part senile, nor the staff seemed particularly happy at this deluge of giggling, chattering teenagers who descended on them to do good – teenagers who had never done a day's housework in their lives. Two nuns and a priest had come along to maintain decorum. Whatever hope the sexes had of mingling together was given short shrift when the nuns took the girls inside to clean the house. The boys were left outside to attend to the grounds, under the supervision of the priest and a very cranky gardener.

Not long after they had been at work, Mala came onto the veranda. "I need two boys to come and move an almirah," she said.

"I'll help," Suraj replied.

But Niresh cried, "Me and Amrith."

He grabbed Amrith's arm and hurried him towards the veranda. Suraj had arrived first, but there were two of them. Mala pretended to look harassed as she glanced from Suraj to Amrith and Niresh. Then, she said ungraciously, "I guess you both can come. I do need two boys."

Niresh grinned at Suraj, who glowered back.

They followed Mala.

"Poor lover-boy," Niresh whispered to Amrith, who smiled sourly.

Suraj was thumping his clenched fist against the palm of his hand.

When the boys had finished in the garden, they lined up at an outdoor pipe to clean off. The ground around the pipe was muddy and so there were two bricks embedded in the soil that they could stand on, as they bent over to use the tap. When Niresh was at the pipe, his feet on the bricks, Suraj came up from behind and gave him a shove. Niresh stepped into the mud and splattered himself. He turned on Suraj, his fists raised. Suraj had already taken up his stance. They began to circle each other. Amrith felt a sickening lurch in his stomach.

The other boys had formed a ring around the combatants, their faces hot with excitement. They called encouragement to Suraj, referring to Niresh as kalu-suddah, black foreigner.

Suraj took a punch at Niresh. He ducked. When he tried to punch back, Suraj stepped aside and Niresh nearly lost his balance. The boys cheered.

They circled again.

"Niresh, come away," Amrith cried, his voice thick in his throat.

Niresh did not even glance in his direction.

They moved around for a while, gauging each other. Then Niresh tried to take another punch at Suraj and missed. Suraj made a jab at Niresh's stomach. His cousin blocked him. In that instant, his face was unguarded. Suraj swiftly changed direction and hit out, catching Niresh squarely on the nose. From the power of his blow, Niresh was flung backwards. He crashed into a bucket and collapsed into the mud.

Amrith cried out.

Suraj pounced on top of Niresh. He straddled his chest, grabbed him by the hair, and hit his head against the ground over and over again. Niresh gasped each time his head struck the dirt. Amrith pushed through the circle and stood, wringing his hands.

Suddenly the priest and the gardener were among them. They grabbed the boys and pulled them apart. The girls, attracted by the noise, had come out of the house. When they saw the state of the boys, some of them shrieked. Amrith helped Niresh to his feet. His nose was bleeding. Mala broke past the others and, with her handkerchief, tried to staunch the blood.

The priest grabbed Suraj by the ear and twisted it until he was bent over. "You are a bloody disgrace, you monkey. Just wait, I'm going to tell your mother." He dragged a sullen Suraj away, who turned to give Mala a look of appeal. She glared at him.

For a moment, Niresh's face shone with triumph, but then, when Mala turned back to him, he quickly changed his expression to pain and pressed her handkerchief to his nose. Leaning slightly on Mala, he allowed himself to be led away. He had actually developed a limp.

The shramadana came to an inglorious end.

When they got home that morning, the women fussed over Niresh, making sure he was comfortably seated in a Planter's chair, plying him with cushions and ice compacts dipped in eau de cologne.

Before lunch, Mrs. Wanigasekera, whom they knew as Aunty Daphne, brought a much-chastened Suraj over to apologize. Aunty Bundle and Uncle Lucky graciously made light of the whole thing, said that boys would be boys, that no permanent damage had been done, that it was just a flash of tempers.

Suraj was made to apologize to Niresh, to shake his hand. His cousin accepted his apology with all the good grace of the victor. For, the moment Mala had seen Suraj enter the courtyard, she had stalked off into the house and did not come back until he was gone.

Throughout all this, Amrith stood by silently. He felt like a supernumerary, watching a drama unfold in which he had no speaking part.

~~~~
~~~~

Amrith decided he had put up with enough. The time had come to assert his will again.

That evening, Aunty Bundle took Niresh to see their family doctor. His cousin had cut his knee on a rusty garden implement during the fight and he needed a tetanus shot. The moment they left, Amrith went looking for Mala. He found her in the girls' room, writing in her diary. He came in without knocking and she hurriedly slipped her diary under a pillow.

"I suppose you have completely forgotten your promise about not monopolizing my cousin," Amrith began abruptly. "You promised –"

"I didn't promise you anything," Mala replied, with equal rancor. "Just leave me alone, Amrith. I have had a very trying day."

"He is *my* cousin," Amrith shouted at her. Without realizing it, he had begun to pace up and down. "Why don't you leave him alone?"

"Akka is right. You are jealous. A jealous baby."

"And you're a . . . a slut."

Mala drew in her breath, appalled.

"You are, you are," Amrith cried. "You think I don't know that you are interested in Niresh? It's so obvious, the way you're throwing yourself at him. I'm surprised Aunty Bundle and Uncle Lucky have not noticed. I wonder what they would think about their daughter breaking their rule."

"I haven't done anything."

"You have. You've encouraged Niresh, led him on."

"Don't be so awful, Amrith. I have not done anything improper. And I have not monopolized your cousin. I only spend time with him when you are at rehearsals."

"What about coming to Kinross yesterday?"

"I was in the courtyard and he asked me."

"You could have said no."

"Well, I wanted to come."

"Yes, so you could throw yourself at him."

"Amrith!"

"He's *my* cousin, *my* relative. It's not fair. You have family and I don't. Why do you want to deny me the one person I have? Do you have any idea what it's like to be me? To grow up alone, with no family who loves you and –"

"Amrith!" Her face filled with dismay. She held her arms out to him. "How can you say that? We love you. We are your family."

"No, you're not. You're not." He was suddenly close to tears.

"I've always thought of you as my brother, Amrith. I have always loved you as my brother. I even love you a little more than I love akka and –"

"Well, I've never thought of you as my sister. Never." He could not stop himself. "I've never loved you as my sister."

She stared at him, horrified, then she burst into tears.

He turned his head away. "No, you are not my sister and I have always-always thought of you, all of you, as strangers. This has never felt like my home."

With that, he turned and stalked out of the room.

Amrith felt no remorse. His anger had been stoked by his own cruelty and it flared and burnt through him. He was helpless in its grip.

When they were getting changed for bed that night, he said to his cousin, "Niresh, I think we should go on a trip.

Just you and I. We should go to Negambo and stay at Uncle Lucky's aquarium. There is a small bungalow there. I'm sure I could get Uncle Lucky to have Soma take us. The watcher could do the cooking. We'd have a great time. It's fantastic at night as you can see the fishermen going out. We could convince them to take us in their boats."

"It sounds like a great idea, Amrith, but you know, I only have six days left and I kind of want to spend it here in Colombo. Do you mind?"

"No, why should I? It's obvious you don't want to spend time with me."

"*Ah,* no, Amrith, come on, that's not true."

"Yes, it is. You think I'm boring and because I am two years younger, you are tired of my company."

Niresh looked at him astounded. "Why are you saying such a thing? I never feel that way." He put his hand on Amrith's shoulder. "This time with you has been the best in my life. I really mean it. Better than anything in Canada."

But no matter what Niresh said, Amrith knew his cousin was in love with Mala. He shrugged his hand off and replied bitterly, "You're lying to me. Just like you lie to everyone else."

He went to his almirah and began to take out some clean clothes.

When he turned around, his cousin was seated on the bed, staring at him. He looked like he had been slapped.

# 17

# Cassio

~~~~~~~~
~~~~~~~~

The next morning, Amrith had a rehearsal and Niresh was going with Aunty Bundle to view the construction of a new hotel on the southern coast.

While they got dressed and had breakfast, Amrith could feel his cousin's gaze on him. He vindictively refused to meet his eye.

As Amrith walked up the front path towards the school buildings, he looked at the clear blue sky and the sunlight that spread its beams over the manicured lawn, with its beds of impatiens and magenta croton bushes. His nerves were stretched to the breaking point.

When he entered the auditorium, Suraj was practicing his monologue onstage, interrupted often by Madam or Fernando so they could correct him and give him some direction. Their voices were exasperated, as Suraj was not a very good actor at all. He had got the part because he looked, as Madam put it in her humorous way, "like a real thug." The rest of the cast were seated in the front rows, watching.

Once Amrith had greeted Madam and Fernando, he went up the steps to take his place on Desdemona's bed. As he crossed the stage, Suraj gave him a haughty glare. It was a warning. Amrith was not to tell anyone about Suraj's humiliation, when he was brought over by his mother and forced to apologize. Amrith raised his eyebrows challengingly and Suraj, out of surprise, dropped his gaze.

Amrith passed him and lay on the bed, his hands folded over his chest.

Suraj began his monologue again. He soon reached the point when Othello approached the sleeping Desdemona and bent down to kiss her. As he leaned close and pretended to do so, he glared at Amrith, who returned his gaze unblinkingly.

Suraj had performed the action of bending so awkwardly that Fernando leapt up on the stage, crying, "For goodness' sake, Wanigasekera! That foot-ruler in your other hand is supposed to represent a lamp. If you tip it like that, you'll set the bed on fire." He came up to them and showed Suraj how to lean over the bed properly.

When Fernando left the stage, Suraj said in a low voice, "Don't think you're a big shot. I could make you very –"

"What? Very what? Do you want to come to my house again like a pariah dog, with your tail between your legs?"

Suraj was silent, out of shock at Amrith's audacity. He began his monologue. He once again reached the point when Othello approached the sleeping Desdemona and leaned down to kiss her. As he bent close over him, he glowered at Amrith, who gazed back unflinchingly.

*"Who's there? Othello?"* Amrith narrowed his eyes at Suraj.

*"Ay, Desdemona,"* Suraj replied, with a stern frown of warning.

*"Will you come to bed, my lord?"* Amrith shrugged ever so slightly to say he didn't give a damn about his warning.

*"Have you prayed tonight, Desdemona?"*

*"Ay, my lord."*

*"If you bethink yourself of any crime*
*Unreconciled as yet to heaven and grace,*
*Solicit for it straight."*

*"Alack, my lord, what may you mean by that?"*

With each line, Amrith and Suraj were ascending higher and higher in their challenge to each other. When they finally reached the part where Othello accused Desdemona of being unfaithful with Cassio, Amrith, rather than beseeching Suraj as he had been directed to do, replied with anger. Suraj raised his ire to match Amrith's and finally they were shouting at each other.

*"Down strumpet,"* Suraj cried.

*"Kill me tomorrow; let me live tonight,"* Amrith yelled back.

*"Nay, and you strive —"*

*"But half an hour!"*

*"Being done, there is no pause."* Suraj rested his hands around Amrith's neck.

Amrith had been directed to lie back and just place his hands on Suraj's arms imploringly, but now he struck out at Suraj's arms. Suraj pressed down harder, trying to hold Amrith. Soon, they were struggling in earnest. A wild surge rushed through Amrith. He lifted his knee, kicked out, and caught Suraj in the stomach. Suraj broke away and Amrith leapt from the bed.

They stood panting, looking at each other.

"De Alwis, Wanigasekera!" Madam and Fernando were hurrying towards the stage. "What on earth is happening?"

"It's Suraj, Madam," Amrith cried, "he tried to strangle me."

"I did not! I was only pretending to do so, but then he began to struggle, Madam, and so I tried to –"

"I did not struggle just for nothing. You were trying to choke me." Amrith came towards the edge of the stage. "And anyway, Madam, why wouldn't Desdemona struggle? It does not make any sense. After all, she loved Othello and was faithful, and he is a bloody fool believing everyone but his own wife. It doesn't make sense that she would lie there like a meek-and-mild type. It's not realistic. *He* has betrayed *her*. She should be furious and fight him as he tries to kill her. Wouldn't anyone put up a fight if they felt they were unjustly treated and –"

"De Alwis!" Madam tapped the edge of the stage. "Stop pacing, De Alwis."

Amrith stood still. He had not realized that he was doing so.

Madam looked at him for a long moment. Then she glanced at Fernando and indicated for him to follow her.

The moment they were out of the auditorium, Suraj said to him, "I'm not done with you."

Amrith did not respond. He was staring after Madam and Fernando with dread.

The other boys had been watching the interaction onstage with great interest, and some of them began to call to Suraj, telling him to deal with Amrith afterwards, to not let a junior cheek him in that way. Yet, Amrith hardly paid these threats any attention, for he noticed that Peries was looking at him, a triumphant smile on his face.

Madam and Fernando soon came back into the auditorium. Their faces were grave as they walked down the aisle towards the stage. Amrith felt a coldness spread through him.

Madam reached the front of the auditorium. She called for Amrith to leave the stage. As he walked down the steps, his legs were trembling. He went and stood in front of her. All the other boys were silent, watching.

"De Alwis," Madam sighed. "Though this is a very difficult decision, I am afraid I have to take the part away from you."

"*Ah*, no, Madam," he pleaded, clasping his hands together. "Please give me one more chance."

She shook her head. "I am afraid I cannot. I warned you last time that this might happen, if you did not improve."

"But, Madam," he said imploringly, "I have learnt my lines; I am putting my best into the part. My very best."

"Yes." She looked at him gently. "I know you are. But, De Alwis, it is not working out. I am sorry. This part is just not meant for you."

"Please, Madam, let me try one more time."

She shook her head. "My mind is made up. You will play Cassio." She ran her hand over her forehead. "Okay, boys," she said in a tired voice, "let's do the scene again." She gestured to Peries. "Go and take your place on the bed."

Madam and Fernando took seats a few rows back.

Amrith continued to stand where he was, numb with shock. Finally, when he saw that Peries was lying on the bed, he went and sat in the front row. As he watched Peries perform his role, a heavy misery took hold of him.

When rehearsals were over, Amrith left ahead of the others. He was waiting in the shaded portico of the main building for his car to arrive, when Suraj bounded down the steps to him.

"*Ah,* Michael Cassio, waiting for your darling Iago to pick you up?"

Amrith looked at him, too miserable to say anything.

Suraj snickered. "Act three, scene three, De Alwis. You'll see yourself in there, no doubt."

"Wanigasekera!"

They turned. Madam and Fernando were standing at the top of the flight of steps. She crooked her finger sternly at him. "Wanigasekera, you don't know the first damn thing about Shakespeare. You're a complete dolt." She turned to Amrith and said, "De Alwis, I see your car is at the gate." She waved her hand for him to be gone.

As he left, he heard her say, "Wanigasekera, I have friends in the theater world who are *that* way inclined, and it's no laughing matter in this country. I don't like such things being ridiculed. Don't ever do that again."

# 18

# The Monsoon Sea

~~~~~~~~
~~~~~~~

At lunch that day, Niresh told the girls about his visit to the construction site, how he had actually been allowed to go up in a crane. He was impressed by what he had seen and especially by Lucien Lindamulagé, who he said was the one of the smartest people he had ever met. Though Niresh appeared to be himself, Amrith noticed that his cousin often glanced at him, anxiously. Amrith refused to meet his eye. Niresh and Mala were responsible for his losing the part of Desdemona. It was their selfishness that had caused him to be angry with Suraj.

That afternoon, they all went to Kinross Beach for a swim. Selvi had suggested the idea at lunch and, since Amrith certainly did not want to be alone with Niresh, he agreed to it.

It seemed like a nice day when they set off from their house but, in the ten minutes it took them to walk to the beach, the weather began to change. By the time they reached Kinross, a rainstorm looked like it would break in the next hour. The sun was a poisonous orange, veiled by clouds. A pinkish-yellow haze hung in the air, making it difficult to see very far down the deserted beach. Distant coconut trees and rocks shimmered like a mirage. Crows whirled and dipped over some carrion, like flecks of ash from a fire. The sea was churned up, a brown color with streaks of bilious green rippling through it.

Something devilish came over Amrith the moment they stepped onto the beach. He stripped down to his trunks and ran towards the sea, ahead of the others. As opposed to hanging back and making his way slowly, like he usually did, he splashed through the water. As soon as it was deep enough, he plunged in with a hoarse cry. He struck out, beating his way against the incoming waves.

When he finally turned around to look back towards the beach, only Mala had come down to the water's edge. Niresh was helping Selvi, whose slipper strap had broken. He was mending it with a safety pin she had given him.

"Amrith," Mala called, wading nervously into the water, "how is it out there?" At the best of times, she was wary of the sea but, with the water all churned up, she was even more uneasy.

"What?" He pretended he had not heard her.

She repeated herself and he cupped his ear to indicate that he still could not hear.

He watched as she swam out to him.

Beyond the beach a train thundered by, its shriek piercing the air.

Mala had reached him. "The water's strange today, isn't it? I hope it doesn't rain while we're here." Since their fight yesterday, she had been trying hard to be nice to him. What he had said about the Manuel-Pillais not being his family had made her feel sorry for him. Seeing the pity in her eyes now, he felt his anger rise a level.

He splashed her face and grinned.

"Hey!" She grinned back, taking this as a sign of forgiveness. She splashed him, too.

They started to circle, bobbing up and down. As if on cue, they began to hit water at each other and soon they could barely see for the spray between them.

Mala accidentally swallowed some of the seawater and she began to cough. "Amrith, surrender, surrender."

"No surrender," he shouted, and continued to slap water, moving closer and closer.

She turned away coughing, "Amrith . . . stop . . . surrender."

He was right in front of her and pushed more and more water. He could not stop himself now, even if he wanted to.

"Amrith!" She backed away. "Stop!"

He sank silently under. In the murky water, he could make out her legs, like the brown tendrils of some seaplant. He swam stealthily towards her. When he was close, he reached out for her legs. At his touch, she kicked out in a flurry of bubbles and tried to get away. But he was too quick for her. He locked his arms around her knees. With a swift tug he brought her under. For a moment, through the clouded water, he could see her hair flying around her face, her mouth gaping like a fish.

In bringing her down, however, he lost his grip. She broke away and disappeared from his sight in a storm of brown foam. Amrith came up to the surface, gasping. He rubbed the water off his face, pushing his hair up his forehead.

Mala backed away from him.

"Amrith, enough is enough! It's not funny anymore."

"Why?" He bobbed towards her. "Why isn't it funny?" He splashed some water at her.

"Stop it, just stop it, men!" Her voice broke.

"*Ah,* don't be such a crybaby. Come on, fight, fight."

"I don't want to."

"Why not?" He splashed her again.

"Just leave me alone," she yelled at him, with sudden anger. "Just leave me alone."

"Fight, fight," he chanted, coming ever nearer.

"What have I done? What? Is it my fault that Niresh loves me and you're jealous because he does?"

The blood thudded to Amrith's head. "What did you say?" he screamed at her. "What did you say?"

"Nothing," she replied, looking away.

"You are a liar." He began to splash her furiously and she had no choice but to splash him, too. "A liar and a slut."

"I am not!" she cried back, her voice cracking. "You're a jealous baby."

Then, with a deep breath, Amrith was underwater. He swam swiftly towards her. When he reached her, he tried to lock his arms around her legs again. She kicked out and caught him in the shoulder. Pain shot through him. It acted as a spur. He darted at her and grasped her calves tightly. She struggled, but he held on, digging his nails into her flesh. He brought her under. Through the stirred-up water he could see her hair spilling out all over, her arms flailing desperately, a look of terror on her face. Her chest was heaving from the water she was swallowing. He held on grimly. Her resistance began to grow weaker; her arms fluttered powerlessly to her sides.

Suddenly strong arms locked around his waist and he was being dragged up out of the water.

"Hey, buddy, buddy," Niresh cried.

Mala surfaced with a strangled sound. She spat out water and began to cough, a loud moaning, wheezing.

Amrith struggled to get out of his cousin's grip, but Niresh was much stronger. He held Amrith tight against his chest.

With her eyes on Amrith as if he were a dangerous animal, Mala backed away. When she was at a sufficient distance, she turned and stumbled towards the shore.

"Let me go, let me go!" Amrith cried, gritting his teeth and struggling to get out of his cousin's grip.

"Take it easy." Niresh released Amrith, now that Mala was safe.

The moment he was free, Amrith lunged into the water and swam away.

"Hey, buddy," Niresh called after him, "why don't you come out for a bit?"

"No!"

"Come on, Amrith."

"No! If you want to go out, go. I'm not stopping you." Amrith swam faster, leaving Niresh behind.

He went out quite far and then turned to look back. Mala was on the beach. Selvi was wiping her off with a towel, bending down to examine the scratches Amrith had made on her sister's calves. Niresh was walking towards them. Selvi wrapped the towel around her sister and, as Mala stood shivering, she began to talk to Niresh, both of them glancing every so often in Amrith's direction.

"I don't care, I just don't care," Amrith muttered to himself, as he treaded water. Yet a sense of shame, of horror, was beginning to take hold of him, as he realized what he had done. He had tried to drown Mala.

Selvi and Niresh waded out and, when the water was deep enough, they swam towards him. Once they reached Amrith, they treaded water, watching him, careful smiles on their faces. They glanced at each other, before Selvi said, "Amrith, it's going to rain any moment now. Why don't you come out?"

Her voice was gentle, almost polite, and he felt even more ashamed. He shook his head stubbornly.

"Come on, buddy," Niresh said pleadingly. "You know, we really need to be getting back, and we can't just leave you here."

"Why not?" he replied haughtily.

"Amrith," Selvi said, losing patience with him, "you better come out. I mean it. Otherwise I'm telling Amma and Appa what happened."

"I don't care. What does it matter what they think? You all are not my family."

Selvi was not fazed by this. "You're being stupid and melodramatic." She turned away. "Suit yourself, I'm not going to hang around here waiting for you." She gestured towards the swollen gray clouds that had thickened above them in the last few minutes. "It's going to pour any minute."

With that, she waded out, indicating for Niresh to follow her.

Amrith watched them swimming towards the beach. "I don't care, I just don't care." He swam out and faced away from the beach. There was an odd band of green light at the horizon, above which the clouds were black and monstrous. A red buoy bounced manically from side to side. When he turned back, the others were no longer there.

Yet, as Amrith looked towards the shore, he realized that he had drifted sideways. He frowned and began to strike out towards land, trying to ride a wave in. But he could get no closer to the beach. He struggled to find a footing in the sand. His feet touched the ground and, in that instant, he felt the current for the first time. He had not been aware of it because he had been floating in the water. Amrith moaned with fear. This had happened to him once before, and he knew better than to fight against it. He had no choice but to wait it out. Amrith watched helplessly as the beach slipped by him, very aware of the pull of the sea beneath. He prayed that the current would continue to move only parallel to the beach and not suddenly change direction, pulling him far out into the ocean.

After what seemed an interminable amount of time, Amrith felt the current ease. He quickly struck out towards the shore, terrified that another rush of current might pick him up and carry him away. When it was too shallow to swim anymore, he got to his feet and floundered through the last stretch of water. He staggered up the beach and collapsed exhausted on the sand. He closed his eyes, his chest heaving from exertion and fear.

Slowly his breath returned to normal. He became aware that it had begun to drizzle. A wave rushed up and broke around him, even though he was far up the beach. He opened his eyes and sat up. The sea was moving into the beach.

Amrith got to his feet and hurried in the direction of the railway lines. He had gone only a few steps when, as if out of nowhere, there was a great wailing and a mighty wind swept down around him. It began to rain, great torrents of water falling from the sky, lashing at his body. The sand on the beach had been stirred by the wind and it rose up, blowing in all directions, stinging his body, getting in his eyes and his mouth. He bent his head, narrowed his burning eyes, and lurched forwards. He was walking into the wind, however, and each step felt as if his feet were weighed down with lead. He stumbled and slipped and finally he fell over a piece of driftwood, sprawling on the sand.

When he struggled to his feet, he saw, not far ahead, a hut that in the good season served as a kiosk, from which a vendor sold slices of pineapple and mango and packets of cashews. He fought his way towards it and, once he reached the hut, he tried the door. It was unlocked. He pushed and it gave inwards, banging against the wall from the force of the wind. Using all his strength, Amrith managed to shut the door behind him and leaned against it, panting.

When he had calmed down, he wiped the water and sand off his face and looked around him. The hut was empty, except for some wooden crates beside the door and a pile of old fishnets in a corner. There was a smell of damp and decay. Amrith sat on the pile of nets. He closed his eyes and leaned his head back against the wall. He could hear the roar of the wind outside, the hammering of the rain on the tin roof above him. The storm was at its height. It was best for him to stay in here until it subsided. Then he could make his way back home.

As Amrith waited, the memory of what he had done to Mala came back to him – the terror in her face, the way her chest had heaved from swallowing salt water. Amrith put his head in his hands and moaned. He thought of how Mala's resistance had grown weaker as he held her under, and he shuddered to think what might have happened if Niresh had not intervened. How could he have done that to his sister? It was as if he had lost sight of himself, as if the Amrith he knew had been absent, replaced by someone else. "*Ah,* no, no," he murmured, and shook his head. "Why did I do that, why?"

Then he recalled what had spurred him on to that final act of anger. It was Mala accusing him of being jealous that Niresh loved her. A thought, a memory, began to come at him from a distance, like an approaching train. It thundered closer and closer and suddenly it was there: that moment, this morning, when Suraj had called him Cassio and asked him if he was waiting for his darling Iago. At the time, Amrith had not paid him any attention, but now he felt a coldness spreading through him as he thought of what Suraj had insinuated. He was referring to Iago's story of how Cassio, in his sleep, took Iago's hand in his, held him tight, kissed him hard on the lips over and over again, and pressed his leg over Iago's thigh.

With a will of its own, Amrith's mind slipped back to that night he had lain awake looking at Niresh, how he had rested his thigh against his, the way his body had flamed with desire; and before that, the time he had got an erection after seeing his cousin naked.

Amrith felt a deep horror seep into him. He loved Niresh in the way a boy loves a girl, or a girl loves a boy. He had been jealous of Mala because of this love and not because Niresh was his cousin. Madam and Fernando had understood the nature of this love; and through them, Suraj, too. People who are "*that* way inclined" was how Madam had referred to this unnatural defect in him.

He closed his eyes and drew his knees to his chest. He tried to think if either Niresh or the girls had guessed the nature of his love. The more he thought about it, the more he felt they did not. The girls, when they called him a jealous baby, simply thought he was being overly possessive of his cousin.

The wind had grown even fiercer, a hollow roar all around him. Looking up, he noticed that one of the sheets of the tin roof had come undone and was beginning to flap up and down dangerously, letting in the rain every time it lifted. Suddenly there was a crash as something slammed into the roof. Amrith yelled out in fear. Another crash followed the first. Amrith cowered in his corner. The wind was beginning to dislodge coconuts from the trees above the kiosk. It was just a matter of time before one fell right through. Amrith knew it could kill him. He struggled to his feet. He had no choice but to leave.

When he opened the door, he paused to take in the sight before him. The sea was massive and swollen. The waves had almost reached the hut by now. He was leaving just in time. Keeping his head down against the rain, Amrith rushed out and ran towards the rocks that separated the beach from the railway lines. He scrambled up the boulders. The rain had made them slippery and he fell backwards a few times, cutting himself, but he finally reached the railway lines. He looked both ways to see if a train was approaching, but it was impossible to tell because of the sheets of rain. He stood uncertainly, until a crack of lightning made him dart across.

Once he was on the other side, he hurried along a laneway that ran parallel to the railway lines. Various streets sloped down to this laneway, and so the rainwater had gushed down the roads and gathered in this path. Soon Amrith was knee-deep in water. His nose wrinkled in disgust as plastic bags and cans and other bits of garbage floated around him. Still, he had no choice but to wade through this filth to get to their road. He lost a slipper and he watched as it floated away and then sank. The toes on his bare foot curled as they touched all sorts of things underwater.

Soon he was past the muddy pool. He hobbled along their road, his bare foot slowing him down. He was halfway up when he heard his name being shouted. He looked ahead and saw Uncle Lucky and his driver, Soma, hurrying down towards him. They were holding pieces of tarp over their heads, which ballooned in the wind like parachutes. When they reached him, Uncle Lucky put his arm around him. "What were you *thinking*, Amrith?" He led him back towards the house.

They entered through the gate to find the rest of the family hovering in the front doorway. Aunty Bundle cried out when she saw him and, the moment he was in the living room, she hugged him, getting her blouse wet. "Child, I was frantic with worry."

Niresh and the girls crowded around him, too, looking guilty.

"Hey, buddy, are you okay?"

"Amrith, I'm so glad to see you."

"Thank God, you're safe."

He stood shivering, not looking at any of them.

Jane-Nona rushed out of the pantry with a cup of hot kothamalli and a towel.

Amrith began to rub himself down, sipping occasionally on the spicy drink of ginger and coriander that was meant to ward off colds.

Now that Amrith had been found, Aunty Bundle and Uncle Lucky turned on the girls, demanding to know what had happened, why they had deserted him. They stood saying nothing, unable to relive the horrible incident.

"You had better tell me." Uncle Lucky eyed them sternly. "Otherwise the consequences will be severe."

The girls looked at each other, then Mala burst out, "Why don't you ask Amrith?" She glared at him. "He's not a child. Didn't he see that a storm was coming up? Why did he remain in the sea?"

Her parents stared at her.

"Young lady —" Aunty Bundle began, but she was cut short by a mighty roar of wind, followed by a deafening sound above them. They all looked up and there, before their very eyes, tiles began to lift off the roof – the very tiles that had been replaced. With a cry, Aunty Bundle and Jane-Nona ran to get the barrel, and Uncle Lucky, the girls, and Niresh rushed around moving furniture out of the way of the falling rain and dust. In the general commotion, Amrith slipped away.

The moment he was in his room, he grabbed a pair of clean shorts and underwear from a pile on the bed and went into the bathroom, closing the door behind him.

He laid his clothes over the towel rail, put down the
toilet seat and sat on it, his head in his hands. "I don't know
what to do," he whispered to himself, "I don't."

When he had changed, he came out of the bathroom to
find Niresh sitting on the side of the bed. He smiled. "Hey,
Amrith."

"*Um* . . . hi."

"Listen," Niresh said, "let's make up, okay?"

Amrith nodded, but he could not meet his cousin's eyes.

"You know, I really don't want us to be mad at each
other," Niresh continued.

"I'm not mad at you."

"Yeah, you are."

"Niresh, I said I am not mad at you."

"Okay, Amrith. Then we've made up?"

"Yes, of course."

Niresh looked at him anxiously and Amrith willed
himself to smile. His cousin mistook his wan smile for a
lack of forgiveness. Without a word, he turned away and
began to flip through a book that lay on the bedside table.

The rain did not let up and, that evening, the family was
forced to gather in the library before dinner, as the living
room could not be used with the hole in the roof. In the
tight confines of the library, the tension between everyone
was palpable. Uncle Lucky and Aunty Bundle were still
angry at the girls for leaving Amrith behind and the girls
were angry at Amrith because he had put them in a spot. At
one point, Selvi said, "I suppose we will have to cancel our

party now, with this new hole in the roof." The girls glared
at Amrith as if he were responsible.

He noticed that his cousin continued to watch him, but
he simply could not meet his eyes. Every time he looked at
Niresh, he writhed inside.

That night, Amrith immediately fell into a deep sleep and
woke late the next morning. Niresh was no longer in the
room. He had left a note saying that he had gone with
Aunty Bundle to look at another project she was working
on. As Amrith lay in his bed, he felt a gray numbness
descend over him. His limbs felt heavy, as if he were ill.
Looking out into the side garden, he saw that the storm was
long over. Everything was lacquered with a harsh late-
morning light.

The tide of his anger had pulled back, leaving him
beached and exhausted.

# 19

## Amrith Appeals
## to the Buddha

〰〰〰〰
〰〰〰〰

The phone rang and rang the next day, and finally Amrith hurried across the courtyard and into the living room to get it. His uncle was calling for Niresh. He went to tell his cousin, who had just showered and changed.

When Niresh came back to the bedroom, he sat on the edge of the bed, staring out through the French windows.

Amrith combed his hair in front of the mirror, pretending not to notice Niresh's black mood. A great distance had come between Amrith and Niresh, between Amrith and everyone, since he had made that realization about himself, two days ago. He felt as if he were in a pit of darkness and there, above, the world carried on with itself in the sunlight.

Finally, when his cousin sighed deeply, Amrith felt compelled to say something. "*Um* . . . is everything alright?"

"It's nothing, Amrith, nothing," Niresh replied sharply. He grabbed his cigarettes and went across the side garden and up to the terrace.

When Niresh did not return, Amrith felt obliged to follow him and see what was wrong. He found Niresh leaning on the balustrade. For the first time since his cousin had come to stay, he was smoking within the compound of their home. Amrith stood a little distance from him. Niresh finished his cigarette and threw the butt over the parapet wall. Then, with a quick movement, he put his head in his hands. "Shit."

"Niresh," Amrith said, with concern, forgetting his own troubles.

"I guess, I guess, talking to my dad, it just hit me. I go back to Canada in three days." He moved away from Amrith, fumbled for another cigarette, and lit it.

Amrith looked at him, appalled. In the midst of all that had gone on, he had forgotten Niresh's imminent departure.

They went to the National Museum that morning. It was an imposing white colonial building set on vast grounds. At the entrance, there was a limestone Buddha that was over a thousand years old. Near the staircase was a tenth-century rock carving of the Goddess Durga.

Once they had paid for their tickets and gone into the first gallery – devoted to clothes worn by the ancient aristocracy of Sri Lanka, along with intricately carved stone decorations from the entrances to ancient temples and palaces – they kept away from each other. When they entered a room, they parted company, going around it in opposite directions. In this way, they made their way through the various galleries of bronze statues, lamps, pottery from the third and fourth centuries, wood and ivory carvings of the seventeenth and nineteenth centuries, the ancient guns and swords used by Sinhalese kings. At one point, Amrith turned from looking at the jewel-encrusted throne of the last king of Kandy – staring at it without really taking it in – to find Niresh was gone.

Amrith found him on a veranda, smoking. He glanced at Amrith and then away. Amrith knew that his cousin would like him to come and sit beside him, but he remained where he was by the veranda post.

"You know," Niresh said, "you are right. I am a liar." He drew on his cigarette deeply and let the smoke escape from his nostrils. "All that stuff I told you about Canada, it was a lie. I don't belong on the football team, and those guys who were supposedly my best friends," he made a contemptuous sound, "they would have nothing to do with me." Niresh gazed out at the garden. "In my school, I am nothing but a freak. A freak and a Paki." He checked to make sure Amrith understood what "Paki" meant. He did because, on a recent trip to England, Aunty Bundle and Uncle Lucky had been subjected to that word by a group of white thugs.

"You want to know a popular joke in my school?" Niresh's mouth twisted bitterly as he spoke, "How do you break a Paki's neck while he's drinking? Slam down the toilet seat."

Amrith was shocked, but he also realized why Niresh was telling him all this. By offering him the truth about his life in Canada, his cousin was hoping that the chasm between them would disappear. Yet, from the depths of his own darkness, Amrith could not summon up any comfort for Niresh, nor cross the distance between them.

〰〰〰
〰〰〰

The day before his cousin was to leave, the family decided to take a trip outstation to Aunty Bundle's favorite Buddhist temple. She wanted to show it to Niresh.

The temple was at the top of a massive rock. A long flight of steps led up to it, flanked by whitewashed balustrades that had pedestals at regular intervals, topped with sculpted lotus pots. Araliya trees spread their branches over the stairs, providing shade. The steps were littered with their crushed blossoms, a strong, sweet smell in the air.

Amrith walked ahead of everyone. At the top of the stairs, he paused to catch his breath, wipe his face with a handkerchief, and look down the steps. At the very bottom, Uncle Lucky and the girls were at one of the kiosks by the entrance. Mala and Selvi were begging him to buy them some bangles, and he was teasing them by complaining that

it was a waste of money. Halfway up the stairs, Aunty
Bundle had stopped to tell Niresh about the history of the
temple and its style of art and sculpture. "Now, son," she
said, gesturing up the steps, "what we are about to see is a
fine example of the Gupta school of art that flourished from
the third to the sixth centuries in India and was brought
over here. It was an amalgamation of two styles. One from
Greece, which came through Afghanistan and which you
will see represented in the classical folds of the Buddha's
robes. The other style was borrowed from the Kushan
Dynasty of Mathura, from which came the rounded – even
slightly female – body of the Buddha, derived from a tradi-
tion of male fertility spirits."

Niresh listened to Aunty Bundle, enthralled.

As Amrith gazed at his cousin, a sense of despair took
hold. Niresh was leaving tomorrow for Canada, and there
was still a great barrier between them. They would part in
coldness. Amrith did not know what to do – how to surmount this barrier; how to get past his own shame and
reach out to his cousin.

He passed through an intricately carved portal into the
deserted compound of the temple, which was on the plateau
of the rock. The ground was mostly stone, with patches of
sand. Bo-trees grew from the cracks in the rocks, the ground
covered with the crisp crackle of leaves. This was the Dry
Zone and there was little other greenery.

The temple was carved out of a cave and, around its
perimeter, there were statues of Hindu deities guarding the

Lord Buddha within. Devotees had placed flowers and incense in front of the statues, asking the gods for favors. Amrith could see the massive form of the Lord Buddha in the shrine room, seated in a pose of meditation. A hole in the top of the cave let in a stream of light that lit the face of the statue. It stared out at him, all-seeing, all-encompassing. Amrith, drawn by the power of the Buddha's gaze, found himself going towards the cave. Before he entered, he removed his shoes as a sign of respect.

The moment he stepped inside the cave-temple, he was surrounded by a great silence. His breath was magnified, and it echoed off the walls. Once his eyes grew accustomed to the gloom, he went forward, feeling the cool rock against the soles of his feet. He stopped in front of the statue and stood gazing up at the serenity of its face.

"Help. Please help me."

Amrith had whispered the words before he quite realized it. He started, as his voice echoed sibilantly off the walls and ceiling. When silence had returned, Amrith, taking courage, said again, "Please help me." This time, strangely, his voice did not echo.

Outside, he could hear Aunty Bundle talking to Niresh as they came past the portal into the temple grounds, the voices of Uncle Lucky and the girls not far behind.

Amrith hurriedly left the cave. He slipped into his shoes and walked to the far parapet wall. He stood, gazing down to the plains below. The monsoon had not arrived in this part of the country yet and everything was parched – the paddy fields a rutted gray mud; the trees stunted and gnarled, denuded of their leaves. The barest trickle of a stream ran through the clay-colored sand of a broad riverbed.

As Amrith looked at the dry landscape, he thought of that story Uncle Lucky had told him about Miss Rani and her connection to his widowed aunt – how the past sometimes offers a way out of a current dilemma. How the past sometimes offers a gift.

Amrith turned away from the parapet wall. Not far from him, Aunty Bundle was showing Niresh a statue of a Hindu god, explaining the symbolic nature of the objects the god carried in his hands. Niresh was listening to her, his mouth open slightly in concentration.

As Amrith looked at his cousin, he thought of the conflict between Uncle Lucky's father and brother, and how Uncle Lucky, carrying the scars of that enmity, had denied his aunt the help she needed. Amrith did not want to end up like Uncle Lucky, regretting his actions for years. No, he did not want that. Despite his own despair, he was going to have to save things between himself and Niresh. And he knew what would help him surmount the barrier that stood between them.

# 20

# Amrith Accepts the "Gift"

~~~~~~
~~~~~~

That night, once Amrith had brushed his teeth and changed into a sarong, he went to his chest of drawers and took out the leather-bound album that contained the photographs of his mother. His cousin was still in the bathroom and so he sat on the bed, waiting for him.

When Niresh came out, he noticed the album and his eyes widened. Amrith patted the bed next to him.

Niresh hesitated, then sat down beside him.

Amrith opened the album to the studio portrait of his mother. "You're right," he said, "my mother was beautiful."

Then, using the photograph to bolster his resolve, he began to tell Niresh about his life on the tea estate and the arrival of Aunty Bundle. There were things that he did not really know, that he could only guess at. For example, he had no idea what made his mother decide to act. He suspected that once Aunty Bundle found out about his mother's situation, she had pushed her to make decisions. This was, he felt, the source of Aunty Bundle's guilt – that, maybe, if she had let things be, at least his mother would be alive today. What Amrith could tell Niresh was the events of that fateful day when he left his mother. He willed himself to do so, to describe, in a shaking voice, the progression of that day.

He had awoken that morning with a start. The sunlight was flooding in, its rays stretching out to the edge of his bed, a thousand dust motes dancing in the beams. Glancing at the clock on his bedside table, he had seen that school had started an hour ago.

He called to his mother, but when she did not respond, he jumped out of bed and went looking for her.

He found her in the window seat of the drawing room, looking out at the mountains. Her knees were drawn to her chest, her hand on her forehead. She did not move when he called her name again, or when he went and stood by her.

"Amrith . . . ," she finally said, turning to him. "You're not going to school today." She touched the side of his face. "Son, we are going to Colombo with Aunty Bundle. For a while."

Then, she told him that they were leaving that evening at five o'clock, once Aunty Bundle had finished her work for the day. He clung to his mother's arm, an incredible joy taking hold. At five o'clock that evening, Aunty Bundle would come in her car and take them away from night sounds and the constant fear of his father.

He wanted to pack right away and they went back to his bedroom. On top of his almirah, there was an old suitcase. His mother took it down. She left it on the floor and went to sit on the edge of his bed, her arms crossed over her stomach, looking out of the window. Amrith hurried about, getting his clothes together. When he called to her, she brushed her hand across her cheek before she came to help him. Together they packed his bag. Once they were done, and the locks were clicked into place, there was nothing more for them to do to get ready.

They went down into the garden and he helped her work on the rosebushes she tended with such loving care. Usually he held the basket with her tools in it. Today, he needed a more vigorous activity that would keep him distracted from his fear that his father might suddenly return. He pestered his mother until she finally allowed him to dig in a spot, to plant some seeds himself. The feel of the cool soil in his hands, the rich smell of it, the various insects and worms that came up as he dug, all kept him so busy that he was surprised when the cook finally came to tell them lunch was ready.

How that last afternoon had stretched. Instead of resting on the veranda, he had been sent to his room. He lay on his bed, watching the clock agonizingly tick away. At one point, he heard a motorcycle on the estate road and ran to the window, terrified that it was his father returning.

By three thirty, the waiting was so unbearable that he got out of bed and put on his traveling clothes. His hands shook as he did so, and it took him a long time to button his shirt. He even put on his socks and shoes. But then there was nothing more to do. He sat on the edge of his bed, listening to the infuriating tick of the clock behind him. The light was beginning to move back towards the window. It seemed fierce, bright, and alive.

He suddenly fell asleep and became lost in a dream. He was walking through a field of tall grass and flowers, which brushed against his legs. He laughed and held his hands out to the sunlight. Then he heard the *hush-hush* of footsteps behind. He looked back. A man was coming towards him, his head lowered. As he drew near, Amrith saw that the man, whom he knew in his dream was his father, had a face that was contorted with hatred, his lips pulled back in a snarl. Amrith tried to run, but the grass was suddenly higher than him and he fought his way through it, lost.

"Amrith, Amrith."

He came to himself with a cry and found his mother bending over him.

"Son," she said, "it is time."

He stared at her for a moment, then sat up, and rubbed his face. It was almost five o'clock. Jumping off his bed, he hurried towards his suitcase. Then he stopped, staring at his mother. She was wearing the same trousers, the same faded cardigan she had on this morning. Her hair was untidy from sleep. "Ammi," he cried to her, "hurry up, hurry up, get dressed. Otherwise we will be late."

She came and knelt before him. He had done his shirt buttons wrong and she fastened them correctly. She drew him into her arms and held him tight. Something gave in her chest. Her hand was in his hair, her nails rasping against his scalp. He pulled away. She was crying.

Then he heard Aunty Bundle's car coming up the road to the bungalow.

"Amrith," his mother said, gripping his arms tightly. "I'm not going with you. I'm sending you to Colombo for a little while with Aunty Bundle."

The car was in their driveway, its wheels crushing the gravel.

"No, Ammi." He backed away. "I'll be good. I promise. I'll do whatever you want."

"Son, son." She rose quickly to her feet and came towards him, "I'm not sending you away because you're bad."

She was holding out her arms to him, but he hurried around the side of the bed. Outside, he could hear the car door slam.

"Amrith, I . . . I need to be alone with your father. He has a drinking sickness. I have to try to help him. I can't do that and take care of you at the same time."

She started to come around the side of the bed. He leapt onto the coverlet and scrambled over to the other side.

He could hear Aunty Bundle calling, "Asha, Asha."

"Ammi," he begged her, "please don't send me away. I want to be with you, no matter what."

"*Ah*, Amrith," she cried, "don't do this to me. It's just for a month or two, that's all. And I will come and visit. Next week. I promise."

"Asha, Asha." Aunty Bundle was coming down the corridor towards his room.

Amrith could also hear the voices of his ayah and the cook in the corridor. He looked around desperately for a way to escape but, at that moment, the door opened and Aunty Bundle walked in. He was trapped between the two women. With a cry, he sank down against a wall and drew his legs to his chest. "Ammi!" he yelled, half in rage, half in despair. "Please don't send me away. Please!"

Then his mother, as if roused from a dream, ran to him, knelt down, and held him fiercely. "Bundle," she said, turning to her friend, "I can't do it. I can't bear to part with him."

"Asha," Aunty Bundle replied, crouching beside her, "it's only for a short time." She touched his mother's shoulder. "Don't weaken now. What you are doing is only out of love for Amrith."

His mother looked from her friend to Amrith. Her hold on him began to loosen. He clung to her even more tightly. "No, Ammi, no."

Aunty Bundle reached out to him, her face full of compassion, but, the moment she touched him, he screamed, "I hate you, I hate you!"

All his affection for Aunty Bundle died in that instant.

His mother pulled his arms off her and stood up, her lips pressed together. Aunty Bundle signaled to the cook, and he came and picked up Amrith. He did not struggle anymore. The only thing he could do was keep his eyes shut against this horror. The cook carried him down the corridor; his mother, Aunty Bundle, and his ayah followed.

Once he was put in the car and the driver started up the engine, Amrith opened his eyes. His mother placed her hand on the car window, the lines in her palm squashed against the glass. She wanted him to rest his palm against hers, but he would not do so.

Instead, staring her in the eyes, he mouthed, *I hate you.*

He saw the disbelief in her face, as if she was sure she could not have understood right. And to make sure she did understand, he mouthed again, *I hate you.*

Those were his final words to his mother. The car inched forward. His mother walked beside it, hugging herself as if she were cold. The car picked up speed and she walked faster. Finally, she was running. Just before the gate, she stopped.

Amrith swung around in his seat and looked through the rear window. His mother was standing in the driveway, her arms rigid by her sides.

That was the last time he saw her.

A few days after he arrived in Colombo, he heard the news. His mother and father had gone for a ride on the motorcycle early one morning. They had left the bungalow just as the sun was rising. As they sped along the estate road, they had reached a dangerous hairpin bend, and that was where the accident occurred. The motorcycle had gone through a short parapet wall on the edge of the bend and crashed down to the plains far below. Nobody knew if it was really an accident and what his mother was doing on the back of that motorcycle in the first place. Where had they been going? Had she gone of her own volition and, if so, had she known what the consequences might be? It was all a mystery.

~~~~
~~~~

Amrith closed the album and put it aside. He was trembling like a leaf. After a moment, Niresh put his arm around Amrith and squeezed his shoulder. "Thank you," Niresh said, "thank you for telling me about my aunt. I wish, so much, that I could have known her." Then he hugged him.

Later, once they had turned out the lights, they both lay with their hands behind their heads, talking. Niresh asked him all the things he wanted to know – what his grandparents had been like, why his father had hated his sister. As Amrith answered him, he was aware of a growing feeling of lightness within. He was aware, for the first time, of the heavy burden of silence he had carried around these past eight years.

At one point, Niresh asked him if he knew anything about his father – what he looked like, what kind of a man he had been. Amrith did not. He told Niresh that his father had also married against his family's wishes and so, after he died, his family had wanted nothing to do with Amrith.

"But don't you wonder about him?" Niresh asked.

Amrith was silent for a moment. "I . . . I guess it's been too painful to think about him at all. And Uncle Lucky is my father now." He turned to his cousin. "Perhaps, one day, I will be interested to know."

That night, Amrith had a strange dream. He was at the very bottom of the sea, but perfectly able to breathe in water. He was involved in the task of pushing an object, many sizes larger than himself, up to the surface. It was his mother's cane chair, grown enormous. The one she had always sat in and that he always found abandoned in his nightmare. He was far smaller than the chair and so it was hard work to move it. But he would not quit, and he swam around, pulling away weeds, dislodging a chair leg that was trapped between two rocks, pushing at the chair with his little shoulders and arms. And gradually it began to rise. Up . . . up . . . up. Towards light.

# 21

# Roses and Silence

~~~~~~
~~~~~~

The next morning at breakfast, the air was heavy with leave-taking. Jane-Nona had made kiri bath for Niresh's last meal with them, as his cousin was particularly fond of this Sri Lankan breakfast of milk rice and curries.

After they had finished eating, Aunty Bundle folded her serviette and stood up. "Niresh, dear, the girls and I will say our good-byes in a few minutes." She glanced at her daughters significantly. They were leaving early on purpose, so Amrith could have the final few moments with his cousin.

Amrith and Niresh waited in the courtyard. Soon, Aunty Bundle and the girls came out to them.

"Well, dear, it's been lovely having you," Aunty Bundle said, touching his shoulder. "Our home is always open to you. Come back and visit."

Niresh pressed his lips together. "Thank you, Aunty."

She hugged him.

"Don't forget how to say hello in Sinhalese," Selvi said, as she hugged him, too. "Next time you come, I will test you on it."

He did his best to smile. "Mama loku gembek."

"Remember us when you are back in your marvelous Canada." Mala held out her hand to him. Their mutual attraction made them slightly formal with each other, but Amrith could tell they were sorry to be parting. "Write occasionally, okay?"

He nodded as he shook her hand. "I promise I will."

Once the women had got into the car, they waved to Niresh and he waved back. The car reversed out into the street. The girls were still waving, but now Aunty Bundle had pulled out a handkerchief and was dabbing her eyes.

The moment the car left, Niresh turned abruptly and hurried to their room. When Amrith came in, Niresh was sitting on the bed by his suitcase, facing away. His shoulders were shaking. Amrith went and sat by him. He rested his hand on his cousin's back. Niresh rubbed the heel of his palm fiercely across his cheek, then gripped his fingers together until he calmed down. "Fucking hell," he said, turning to Amrith with a lopsided grin, "I'm even out of smokes."

After a moment, Niresh picked up his suitcase and they went towards the door.

"Wait," Niresh said softly. "I want to remember this room."

He stood for a moment looking around, taking in everything: the bed, the drawers, the almirah, the side chair, the French windows with their lace curtains blowing in the breeze. He closed his eyes, as if imprinting it all in his mind; as if storing it away as a future comfort. Then he nodded to Amrith.

Uncle Lucky was in the courtyard, waiting by the car. He was giving Niresh a lift to the hotel.

Niresh turned to Amrith with a brave smile. "Thank you. I'll never forget the time I've spent with you." He put down his suitcase and placed his hands on Amrith's shoulders. "Now that we've found each other, let's never lose touch, *eh*. You'll write, won't you?"

Amrith nodded.

Then Niresh held him tight and Amrith, too, put his arms around his cousin. They pulled apart, after a moment, both a little embarrassed.

Niresh held up his hand. "One last joke. What happens when you cross a centipede and a parrot?"

"I don't know."

"You get a walkie-talkie."

Amrith smiled as best he could. His cousin had cracked that joke before.

Niresh got into the car and it reversed out into the road. All the while he was staring at Amrith, who stared back.

Then his cousin was gone.

Amrith stood in the courtyard, listening to the car go up the road, and soon he could hear it no more. A crow called loudly from the bougainvillea and a squirrel scampered in the jak tree. Someone was burning leaves a few houses down, an acrid smell in the air. In the distance, a passing train whistled mournfully.

He did not know what to do with himself. He went to his room and sat on the edge of his bed, then lay with his hands behind his head. After a while, he got up and went out of the French windows, across the side garden, and up the terrace steps. He let himself into the aviary, but then did not have the spirit to attend to his birds. He just stood in there as the birds flew around him.

By the end of the morning, Amrith could not bear to be home anymore; could not bear the quiet and emptiness that reminded him of Niresh. He asked Aunty Bundle to drop him off at Aunt Wilhelmina's for the afternoon. He was hoping that being in the old lady's house, surrounded by all her beautiful things, would bring him some peace.

Aunt Wilhelmina was at her usual bridge game on the front veranda. She was delighted to see Amrith and, as he came up the front steps, she beckoned him towards her chair. "*Ah,* child, how nice to have you back. My ornaments are in a dreadful state." She pressed his arm and looked at him, her head to one side. "Your cousin left today?"

He nodded.

"Yes, I hear your uncle finally concluded the sale of Sanasuma." She glanced at the other dowagers, who looked back at her significantly, then she simpered, "And he was in such a mighty hurry to get his hands on some money, that he let the property go for far less than it was worth."

"Mervin was always too greedy for his own good," Lady Rajapakse declared, as she dealt the cards.

"Greedy and foolish," Mrs. Zarina Akbarally added, as she took up her cards.

"He is off to Canada with no idea how thoroughly he has been bamboozled," Mrs. Jayalukshmi Coomaraswamy said, and all four old ladies tittered in delight.

Aunt Wilhelmina led Amrith through the drawing room and dining room, waiting for him to make his choice from her glass-fronted cabinets. He picked the one containing her porcelain ornaments. She rang for her retainer, Ramu, and told him to bring some rags and a feather duster. Amrith was left to his work with fish patties and a glass of mixed-fruit cordial.

As he took out the ornaments and began to carefully dust and clean them, the loss of his cousin sat heavy in his stomach.

That evening, when Uncle Lucky got back from the office, he summoned Amrith to the master bedroom.

He came in to find Uncle Lucky seated on the edge of a chair, peeling off his socks. He threw them into the dirty-clothes basket and began to undo his tie. "Amrith, your typing has been thoroughly neglected, *nah*. An important skill for your future. I don't approve, as you know, of people passing their holidays doing nothing-nothing. So, now that your cousin is gone, it is time to start spending the mornings in my office again."

Amrith nodded. He was relieved to have something to occupy his time.

~~~~

When Amrith was back in the office in front of the typewriter, he thought how incredible it was that, just a short time ago, when he had first begun his typing exercises, he had not known his cousin. It seemed as if years had passed since then. How odd it was – the way that life could gather in stillness and then burst its banks, flowing forward with such rapidity.

Amrith came home for lunch to find his room had been tidied up. The extra set of pillows was removed and Jane-Nona had redistributed his clothes to all the shelves of his almirah. In the bathroom, Niresh's towels were gone. It was as if his cousin had never been here.

That night, after he got into bed and turned the lights off, he longed for Niresh's presence next to him.

While Amrith grieved the loss of his cousin, however, the world around him carried on.

He kept attending rehearsals for *Othello* and putting up with playing Cassio, a role that would not bring him any accolades. Yet, losing Desdemona to Peries seemed less painful now. Amrith's mind was too taken up with missing Niresh to really care anymore. As he sat in the auditorium and watched his rival do the role, he conceded that Peries was better at it than he had ever been. Perhaps Madam was right all along – this part was just not meant for him.

There were now four days until Mala and Selvi's party and the living room roof still had a gaping hole in it. The party might have to be canceled after all.

Yet, just when they had decided to inform all the guests that the party was called off, the family was at lunch one afternoon, when they heard a banging on the gate and a voice calling out, "Baby-Hamu, we have arrived."

The dogs rushed out barking, and Aunty Bundle leapt to her feet, crying, "*Ah,* they're here! They're here!"

She hurried out, followed by Uncle Lucky, Amrith, and the girls.

Jane-Nona was opening the gate and the men trooped into the courtyard – Gineris and his "boys," who were practically middle-aged men now. Gineris wore his gray hair in the traditional way, pulled into a topknot and held in place by a carved tortoiseshell comb. He came forward and tried to touch Aunty Bundle's feet in a gesture of respect. She stopped him. He still referred to her as Baby-Hamu, as he had been coming to her family since she was a child.

Jane-Nona, who had gone back to the kitchen, returned bearing a tray with cups of steaming milky tea on it. While the men sipped their tea, she and Aunty Bundle inquired about their families, congratulated them on the birth of grandchildren and marriages, commiserated with them over deaths and illnesses.

"I knew you would not let me down, Gineris," Aunty Bundle said, patting the old man on the shoulder. "Others," she said, glancing at her husband, "might have had their doubts, but I never did."

"*Ah,* Baby-Hamu," he replied, giving her a toothless grin, "how could I fail you?"

When they had finished their tea, Aunty Bundle led the roofers into the living room to look at the damage. Gineris could tell right away that another roofer had attempted to lay down tiles and he grimaced and said, with a sidelong glance at Uncle Lucky, "These modern roof-baases, with all their machinery. Our ancient Sri Lankan ways are always the best." He clapped his hands at his sons. "Now, let us get to work."

The roof was soon repaired and arrangements for the party sped ahead.

The gardener arrived to work on the gardens and Meenukshi, the woman who cleaned for them, came to polish the floors of the living and dining rooms. The furniture had to be moved. Amrith and the gardener lifted the chairs, tables, bureaus, and antique chests into the library, master bedroom, and the girls' room. Except for the dining table, the rest of the furniture would remain displaced, even after the floors were polished. The living room was going to be used for dancing. While Amrith was assisting the gardener, Mala and Selvi helped Meenukshi take down the curtains so they could be sent to the laundry. The bare floors of the living room were suddenly flooded with light.

Since it was not crowded with furniture, the girls set themselves up in Amrith's room to make the decorations for the party. They sat on a mat, cutting hearts out of red bristol board, making pink tissue-paper roses, bickering over some minor point about streamers and balloons.

They had not forgotten Niresh, but Amrith saw that they had put his cousin's departure behind them.

The smell of polish and freshly cut grass and the furniture piled in the various rooms usually created a giddy anticipation in Amrith, a happy sense of their lives turned upside down. But now he felt despondent that Niresh was not here to share in the excitement.

Yet, something else was troubling Amrith. The arrival of Lucien Lindamulagé, one evening, brought it to the fore.

Since Niresh's departure, Amrith had taken to riding his bicycle more often down to the beach. He would go for long walks, lost in gloomy thought, or just sit on a rock, aimlessly flinging pebbles and shells out to sea. The monsoon appeared to be over. The sea was pulling back, leaving behind greater stretches of beach each day. The water had returned to a shimmering turquoise, like blue silk shot through with threads of silver.

He came home from one of these excursions to find the old man having tea with Aunty Bundle in the courtyard. He was seated in his usual manner in a Planter's chair, his legs drawn up to his chest, his feet tucked under his sarong. They were talking about the progress of the new hotel and Lucien Lindamulagé's eyes sparkled with enthusiasm as he described his ideas for the interior, gesturing broadly to explain his vision.

As Amrith looked at the old man, he remembered the scandal surrounding his male secretaries, how Uncle Lucky had warned his wife that what the architect did was illegal; how Aunty Bundle had refused to believe her friend was depraved in that way, though it was clear she was saddened and troubled by the possibility; how boys in his school had referred to the old man as a "ponnaya."

Lucien Lindamulagé had seen Amrith now and he broke off his description. "*Ah,* my boy!" he cried out, and beckoned him over.

As Amrith leaned his bicycle against the wall, he wished he had stayed away longer and missed the old man's visit. His heart was heavy as he went towards Lucien Lindamulagé.

"*Ah,* dear boy, I'm still keeping my eye open for that male mynah bird." The architect reached out and squeezed his arm affectionately.

Amrith felt a deep shudder within. It was all he could do to stop himself from pulling his arm away.

"And how is that demoness Kuveni? Still not talking?" Lucien Lindamulagé asked.

Amrith nodded. He suddenly could not bear to be around this man, whom he had known since childhood. At the first opportunity, he excused himself and went to his room.

The moment he closed the door, he sat on his bed and breathed out, as if he had been holding his breath in all this time. He put his head in his hands and clutched at his hair, a strangled sound escaping from between his gritted teeth. A ponnaya – that was what he was, a ponnaya. He did not know what to do about this thing within him, where to turn, who to appeal to for comfort. He felt the burden of his silence choking him.

That night, Amrith had his old nightmare. He ran up the estate road, in through the gates, and around the side of the house to the veranda. This time, however, he found his mother seated in her chair. She smiled at him and shook her head, as if to say, "Now what were you so worried about, son?"

When Amrith awoke, he knew what he must do.

~~~~~~

His mother's grave had not been visited in a little while. The grass was high on it, and the tombstone was splattered with bird droppings. Amrith was aware that there was an outdoor tap nearby. He went along a path among the graves until he came to the little shed where the groundskeeper kept his implements. There was a watering can by the tap and he filled it up and carried it back to his mother's grave. He knelt down beside the tombstone. Taking out his handkerchief, he dipped it in the water and began to scrub away at the bird droppings. In the distance, he could see smoke

rising up from a crematorium. Along one of the main thor-
oughfares of the cemetery, a hearse moved slowly, followed
by mourners singing a hymn.

When the stone was clean, Amrith sat back on his
haunches and looked at his mother's name for a long time.
Then, with a quick glance around to make sure he was
alone, he leaned forward till his lips were inches from the
stone. He whispered, "I am . . . ," but he could not continue, for he did not know a decent word to describe
himself. And he refused to use "ponnaya." Finally, he
leaned closer and whispered, "I am . . . different."

Just by saying it out loud, just by admitting that it was
so, Amrith felt the burden of his secret ease a little. It was all
he could do for now. He would have to learn to live with
this knowledge of himself. He would have to teach himself
to be his own best friend, his own confidant and guide. The
hope he held out to himself was that, one day, there would
be somebody else he could share this secret with. But for
now he must remain silent.

Later, as Amrith made his way towards the entrance,
he passed through the old British part of the graveyard.
As he looked at the broken tombstones in the knee-high
grass, he made a vow that this would never happen to his
mother's grave.

That evening, Lucien Lindamulagé came to call again. He
had come specially to see Amrith, to tell him that he had
heard of a male mynah that was for sale. They went up to
the aviary to look at Kuveni. As they climbed the stairs,

Lucien Lindamulagé took Amrith's arm for support, and this time Amrith did not shudder at his touch.

When they were in the aviary, Amrith watched Kuveni busily pecking away at the mango he had brought. She paused occasionally to dart a glance at the budgerigars that hovered nearby, making a few threatening movements towards them if they dared come too close. It struck Amrith that Kuveni had never resorted to feather-plucking, or any other signs of anxiety and depression. She seemed perfectly content to be alone. Perfectly content to remain silent. And he realized that he had grown to like her silence. He was not sure, at all, that he wanted another mynah.

"You know, Uncle," he said, turning to Lucien Lindamulagé, "I think we'll leave Kuveni as she is, for now."

Lucien Lindamulagé looked at him over the top of his glasses. "Very well, my boy, let us leave it at that."

〰〰〰

The day of the party was beautiful, a clear blue sky and a salty breeze blowing in from the sea.

Amrith did not go to the office that morning. There was too much to do. The gardener and Meenukshi arrived before breakfast. They would stay through the night to help, and even sleep over. By nine o'clock in the morning, the tradesmen had started to deliver their merchandise.

The Elephant House van dropped off crates of aerated waters and huge blocks of sawdust-covered ice, which the gardener immediately split with an axe and Meenukshi put into coolers. The chairs arrived from Quickshaw's. Amrith and the girls helped the gardener set them up around the courtyard. Then there was the decorating of the living room to be done, with the bristle-board hearts, streamers, bows, tissue-paper roses, and balloons. The curtains were delivered from the laundry and the sisters held up the ends as Meenukshi got on a chair and hooked them to the rods. Amrith and the gardener carried out the dining table to a corner of the courtyard and spread a tablecloth over it. He dug out the Christmas lights, which the gardener strung through the jak tree in the courtyard.

Aunty Bundle arrived at lunch with the girls' dresses and time was wasted as they put them on and looked at themselves in the mirror. In the afternoon, Aunty Bundle stayed home. She sent Amrith with Mendis to do the last errands – pick up the birthday cakes and patties from Perera and Sons, go to Bombay Sweet Mart for more Mixture, and make a quick stop at Elephant House for another crate of aerated waters.

Time, as it always did when moving towards a deadline, sped up and when Amrith got back, it was five o'clock. He was helping unload the car, when Aunt Wilhelmina arrived. She swept in wearing a yellow linen dress and, as usual, matching handbag, gloves, hat, and shoes.

Aunty Bundle seated her in the courtyard and called on Jane-Nona to bring the old lady a drink and some patties. Aunt Wilhelmina, once she had taken a sip of her cordial and a nibble of a patty, beckoned the girls forward. Amrith went too, eager to see what they were getting. Her first gift was to Mala – fifty rupees to buy whatever she wanted. Next it was Selvi's turn and, since this was her sixteenth birthday, she received a Ceylon Stones jewelry set – a broach, necklace, earrings, and bracelet all done in star sapphires, star rubies, moonstones, garnets, and topazes.

They all gathered around Selvi to admire her gift, exclaiming over how pretty the settings were.

Aunt Wilhelmina cleared her throat loudly. "I am not done yet. I have one more gift." She waited until she had their attention before she brought out a scroll of paper tied with a red ribbon. "This is for Amrith."

He stared at her in astonishment.

"Come, child, open it up."

He took the scroll and pulled off the ribbon. Aunty Bundle and the girls crowded around him. When he unrolled the sheet of paper, he stared at it in puzzlement. It was an official-looking document in a complicated Sinhalese that he could not understand. Aunty Bundle, however, could read it and, with a cry, she snatched the document away from Amrith and began to pore over it, her eyes growing wider and wider. She finally lowered the paper. "Amrith," she said, in a hushed voice, "it's the deed for Sanasuma. In your name."

They all turned to stare at Aunt Wilhelmina.

"Well," the old lady said with a sniff, "I was not about to stand by and let that blackguard, Mervin, rob our Amrith of his inheritance."

She crooked her finger at him and touched her cheek, a small smile on her face. "Now, young man, show some gratitude."

He longed to rush over and hug her tight, but he knew that she belonged to a generation where such behavior was considered improper. So he dutifully kissed her on both cheeks, whispering, "Thank you, Aunt Wilhelmina."

Aunty Bundle, however, had no such compunction. She flung her arms around her aunt, knocking the old lady's hat off, and cried with girlish exuberance, "Aunt Wilhelmina, you are such a darling!"

"Goodness, Bundle," her aunt said, with a surprised laugh. "You really are forgetting yourself."

～～～
～～～

The guests would soon be arriving and, once Aunt Wilhelmina had gone, the family scattered to their rooms to have their showers and get dressed. Amrith found it impossible to tear himself away from the deed. He lay on his bed, his hands cupping his chin, as he gazed at the document. It seemed unbelievable that here, before him, was a piece of ancestral property – a real link to his past, to his mother. He found himself remembering that eucalyptus tree on which Aunty Bundle and his mother had carved their names. One day, he would take his cousin to Sanasuma and they would carve their names below those of the two women. *Amrith and Niresh. Best Friends.*

Later, once Amrith had changed and was buttoning up his new shirt, Aunty Bundle knocked on his door and came in. She was wearing a purple silk sari with a gold border.

"Son," she said, "are you alright? I've noticed you seem sad since Niresh left." She straightened the collar of his shirt and pushed back the hair on his forehead. "I have been thinking about something. There is a very nice group of young men and women doing shows at the Lionel Wendt Theater, these days. I know some of them. Would you like to get involved? Perhaps you might make a few friends there."

"*Um* . . . let me think about it, Aunty."

"Well, you decide and let me know, dear." She gave him a worried glance.

"*Um* . . . Aunty?"

"Yes, dear."

"I . . . I've been thinking about something." He looked down at his hands. "You know, Ammi always loved roses. She . . . she so enjoyed growing them on the estate. So I was thinking that I would like to plant some roses around her grave."

"Amrith," she said, placing her hands on his shoulders, "you *do* remember."

He held her gaze for a long moment and then nodded. "I never forgot, Aunty."

Outside, they could hear the gardener banging away at something, Jane-Nona calling for Meenukshi to help her.

"Well, Amrith," Aunty Bundle said, taking her hands off his shoulders. She looked at him with a little smile, her head to one side. "You do realize that roses need a lot of tending in our tropical climate."

"Yes, Aunty," he said, smiling back at her, "I do."

"Well, that's settled then. Roses it will be." Aunty Bundle rubbed her hands together, her eyes sparkling. "I know just the place to get them. Aunt Wilhelmina's friend Lady Rajapakse is an avid horticulturalist and has, evidently, bred a species of roses that grows well in our Colombo soil. Let's go tomorrow and see if she will give us some cuttings."

Uncle Lucky was calling to Aunty Bundle from the courtyard. She turned to leave and then, on impulse, came back and hugged Amrith tightly. "I'm so glad, son, so glad." When she pulled away, there were tears running down her cheeks. She shook her head, laughing. "Child-child, me and my waterworks."

He laughed too. She took out a handkerchief that was tucked in her sari blouse and blew her nose.

"Bundle!" Uncle Lucky called, "where are you, men?"

"I'm here, Lucky, I'm here." She patted Amrith's arm and bustled towards the door.

Amrith looked after Aunty Bundle and he wondered how he had ever held such resentment against her all these years.

Soon, there was a shriek of female voices in the court-yard, a crying of greetings. Two of the SNOTs had arrived early, evidently to help out. In the living room, someone had put on an Olivia Newton-John record. Amrith knew he could not stay in his room much longer. He stood in front of the mirror, tucked his shirt in, folded up the sleeves, and adjusted the shoulders. He went to his dresser, took out a handkerchief, and dabbed some aftershave on his neck. As he passed the mirror, on his way out, he glanced one last time at his reflection. He thought of his cousin and he let himself imagine that, at this very moment, Niresh was wearing his copy of the shirt, all those miles away in Canada.

There was further shrieking and calling out of greetings as more of the girls' friends arrived. Amrith, with a small smile to himself in the mirror, went out to join the party.

# Acknowledgments

My first and greatest thanks goes to Kathy Lowinger, who cast her silver net into the turbulent monsoon sea of my words and drew in this novel. As always, my love and gratitude to my partner, Andrew Champion, who, with his editorial advice, good sense, and love, steered me through the writing of this book. Thanks also to Catherine Bush, Judy Fong Bates, and Rishika Williams for invaluable advice on various drafts of this novel. Many thanks to my agent, Bruce Westwood, for all his support; to Natasha Daneman, who looks after my interests with such care and affection; and to Sue Tate at Tundra Books for her meticulous copyediting. I am indebted to the Canada Council for the Arts, the Ontario Arts Council, and the Toronto Arts Council for their financial assistance.